Acclaim

of CHARLES W

"No one writes a better crime novel than Charles Willeford."
— *Elmore Leonard*

"Extraordinarily winning…Pure pleasure…Mr. Willeford never puts a foot wrong."
— *The New Yorker*

"If you are looking for a master's insight into the humid decadence of South Florida and its polyglot tribes, nobody does that as well as Mr. Willeford."
— *New York Times Book Review*

"Willeford builds up enormous tension—you are compelled to keep reading."
— *Philadelphia Inquirer*

"Absolutely brilliant in every regard."
— *Stanley Ellin*

"Bone-deep satire…terrific."
— *Publishers Weekly*

"A marvelous read."
— *Harry Crews*

"A top-notch crime novel…both tough and funny."
— *Washington Post*

"Lean and hard and brand-new."
— *Donald E. Westlake*

Mel looked past my shoulder across the room, raised his chin. "That's Mrs. Chatham, the blonde talking to Mrs. Barnes."

Turning on the stool, I spotted her easily. Mrs. Chatham was wearing a red-silk cocktail gown that looked as if it had been sewn onto her body. Her face and shoulders were evenly tanned, and her long tawny hair was like a mane down her back.

"She's a real beauty, Mel."

"Now she is, but not for long. She's a lush, Richard. In about one minute she'll be over at the bar asking for a double-martini."

"That's no indication that she's a lush. Maybe she just likes gin."

"There's worse lushes around here, I got to give her that," Mel confided darkly...

UNDERSTUDY
for DEATH

by **Charles Willeford**

A HARD CASE CRIME NOVEL

A HARD CASE CRIME BOOK
(HCC-134)
First Hard Case Crime edition: July 2018

Published by

Titan Books
A division of Titan Publishing Group Ltd
144 Southwark Street
London SE1 0UP

in collaboration with Winterfall LLC

Print edition ISBN 978-1-78565-698-9
E-book ISBN 978-1-78565-690-3

Design direction by Max Phillips
www.maxphillips.net

Typeset by Swordsmith Productions

The name "Hard Case Crime" and the Hard Case Crime logo are trademarks of Winterfall LLC. Hard Case Crime books are selected and edited by Charles Ardai.

Printed in the United States of America

Visit us on the web at www.HardCaseCrime.com

For Bill Bittner

in
this dilemma
…what can a
woman do?

☛ LAKE SPRINGS, *city, Florida; altitude 18 feet, on the Florida East Coast Railroad; with airline service. The city is a southern Florida distributing point for agricultural and dairy products. Manufactures include sports clothing, electronics accessories, pharmaceuticals and tiles. Lake Springs, for which the city was named, is noted for its opaque waters, and is a popular attraction for tourists. There is an alligator farm, a zoo (animals indigenous to Florida only) and a Seminole Indian museum. Incorporated in 1906; it has a commission-manager form of government. Pop. (1950) 37,611.*

Chapter One

A well-to-do Lake Springs matron, Mrs. Marion C. Huneker, 30, after leaving a farewell note addressed to her husband, Mr. Jack L. Huneker, 36, president of the local Huneker Concrete Block & Ornamental Iron Co., fatally shot her two small children and herself last night.

Mrs. Huneker died without regaining consciousness in the ambulance on the way to the hospital from the self-inflicted head wound from her husband's .22 cal. Colt Woodsman semi-automatic pistol. Mr. Huneker had purchased the pistol a month ago, he said, to shoot rats that were increasing at his storage sheds at 3409 Melvin Rd. A sales slip found on the dresser in Mrs. Huneker's death bedroom revealed that the suicidal-bent matron had purchased a box of .22 long rifle shells from the Outdoor Sporting Equipment Store yesterday morning. The pistol was discovered by Detective Charles G. Riddell, in charge of the investigation, beneath the bedside table near the dead woman's right, outstretched hand.

Mr. Ralph Blaiksee, a salesman at the Outdoor Sporting Equipment Store, in speaking to Detective Riddell confirmed the sale of the shells to Mrs. Huneker.

"If I had known Mrs. Huneker was going to shoot herself and her two children," Mr. Blaiksee told Detective Riddell, "I wouldn't have sold them to her."

While Mrs. Huneker was shooting her two children and herself at home, 1406 Lake Shore Drive, in the exclusive residential district of the city, her husband was downtown buying liquor at Ben's Package Store for a party the couple was scheduled to give this coming Saturday evening. Her husband arrived home at approximately 8:45 P.M. last night.

Detective Riddell told this reporter that Huneker walked into the house and found his wife unconscious on their double-bed. Due to the small wound beneath her hair left by the small-calibre bullet he did not know that she had shot herself. But when he could not make her regain consciousness he called the emergency number of St. Catherine's Hospital and ordered an ambulance.

A moment later he found the suicide note on the bedroom dressing table:

THE DEATH NOTE

I cannot stand it any longer. I don't belong and neither do my children. Television is more important than we are. Everything is nothing.

Every day the walls move in closer and closer and I am being smothered. My life goes on in the same way no matter how I try. This is the only way I know to change it.

Although I may not go to Heaven, at least my two babies will go before they have sinned in the eyes of God.

The note, written with a round firm hand in ball-point pencil on a piece of light gray monogrammed stationery, was signed Marion Casselli; Mrs. Huneker's maiden name.

After reading the suicide note the distraught and bewildered husband began a frantic search for his two children.

He found his daughter, Kathy, 6, beneath her bed where she had evidently tried to hide from her mother. The child was dead.

Mr. Huneker's son, Antonio, 8, was not inside the house. The husband continued his search outside and found the boy in a treehouse in the backyard that overlooked the lake. The treehouse had been built a few weeks ago by Antonio and other members of his Cub Scout Pack No. 8. The light of a small pencil flashlight shining in the branches of the tree attracted Mr. Huneker to the treehouse. There was blood on the cross-board steps leading up to the crude structure, and Detective Riddell surmised that the boy was probably shot elsewhere, and then climbed to the treehouse platform to die. When his father found him, Antonio was dead.

Mr. Huneker could give the police no reason for the murder-suicide. His wife had not shown any signs of despondency, and had been looking forward eagerly to the party they had planned for the weekend.

The family had eaten dinner early, Mr. Huneker stated, and his wife had been in good spirits during the meal and afterwards. When he left the house after dinner to go downtown, Mrs. Huneker had been singing in the kitchen to herself, he said. Both of his children had been watching their favorite television program, "The Restless Gun."

According to neighbors, the late Mrs. Huneker was very active in the community. She was the Den Mother of Cub Scout Pack No. 8, and a member of the Jaycees' Wives Club, The Beachcomber's Club, The Lake Shore Home & Garden Club, and on the Flower Arranging Committee of The Beachcomber's Club. She was enrolled in the Creative Writing class at the Adult Education Center, and was also a member of the Roman Catholic Church of the Sacred Heart.

One neighbor stated that she and Mrs. Huneker had gone to the courthouse a few months back to register for jury duty, but that neither of them had served as yet. The same neighbor said that she had collaborated with Mrs. Huneker on a letter to the City Commission a few weeks ago complaining about the inadequate lighting system along Lake Shore Drive.

--30--

Without rereading the copy I gathered the four double-spaced, typed sheets of paper together and took them into the Managing Editor's office. J.C. Curtis, the Managing Editor of the Lake Springs *Morning News* and *Evening Press* (yes, both papers), picked up his soft, crumbly, No. 1 pencil and snatched rudely for the copy.

I considered this a grievous fault of J.C.'s, but I imagine all M.E.'s are about the same. They can't read anything without a pencil in their hand. As I stood patiently beside J.C.'s desk I could visualize this little guy in his lonely hotel room, his pencil clutched in his fingers, reading a Gideon Bible—crossing out this word, substituting a better one, scratching through inept sentences, and cutting the long paragraphs down to size. His size.

J.C. Curtis held the unshakable opinion that no paragraph could possibly be longer than three sentences. And if a sentence happened to be overly long, he delivered a dull, standard lecture about it. I had had several of these.

The M.E. marked the first paragraph for a two-column, ten-point lead, and flicked in new paragraph angles with his soft pencil as he read. He raised his head and glared at me through the top half of his bifocals with a baffled look of stupefaction on his narrow face.

"I'll swear to God, Hudson," he said impatiently, "I just don't know about you sometimes. I don't know whether you write this way to make me sore, or whether you really don't know any better."

"What's the matter this time?" I said sullenly.

"This beautiful little gem," he said mordantly. " 'If I had known Mrs. Huneker was going to shoot herself and her two children I wouldn't have sold them to her.' " He said this with an air of outraged piety, and I had to laugh.

"That's exactly what he said," I grinned.

"I don't doubt it, but can't you see that it makes that poor salesman sound like a damned fool?"

"He is a damned fool."

"You don't have to prove it to the public. Let them find out for themselves. And besides, the Outdoor Sporting Equipment is an advertiser." His pencil blackened the offending quote.

The next line to go was the neighbor's remark concerning the drafting of a letter to the city commissioners. I didn't particularly care, but I did wonder why. "Does a letter complaining about poor lighting make a fool out of the neighbor?"

"This is an obvious lie." J.C. shrugged. "You were around

asking questions, and she saw an opportunity to get in a bad word for the street lights, that's all. You're skeptical enough about some things, Hudson, but this is a manifest case of gullibility, and you ought to know better."

"That's the truth, Mr. Curtis. The lighting really could be improved along Lake Shore Drive. The street lights in that section are three and four blocks apart."

"In that case, it's an item for the editorial page, not for a story on suicide. Otherwise, it'll do. Give the story to Harris and tell him to put a banner on it."

I picked up the copy and J.C. said: "And tell Harris to wait another half-hour before he puts it on the wire so Miami won't have it in time for their first morning editions. Then come back in here, Hudson, I want to talk to you."

I relayed J.C.'s message to Harris, *Morning News* City Editor and Copy Chief, and watched over his hunched shoulder as he read rapidly through the copy. Without even pausing to think for a moment he quickly block-printed a banner head on a narrow strip of white paper, and paper-clipped it to the story.

Mother Blasts Self, 2 Kids, Blames TV

The head wasn't absolutely accurate, but set in 96 point Tempo Heavy, it would sell a lot of newspapers. And it was exactly in line with the paper's policy to knock television at every opportunity, except when we were ignoring the medium altogether. Neither one of the papers, morning or evening, ran the local television listings, and Lake Springs had two stations. A little nervous—I'd been goofing off quite a bit lately—I drifted back to the M.E.'s office.

"Shut the door and sit down, Hudson," J.C. said, rolling his yellow pencil between his palms.

"Yes, sir." After I sat down I looked at him, but there wasn't much to see. J.C. had one of those deadpan faces, and even when he raised his voice in violent anger, which he did once in awhile, his expression rarely changed. A small middle-aged man, he made the word "wizened" his very own. His pale bald head, ridiculously hooked nose and round thick glasses always reminded me of a lifelike, expertly stuffed falcon. Dave Finney, who used my desk in the daytime, and who was my counterpart on the *Evening Press,* told me once, after a racking J.C. had given him, that our joint Managing Editor resembled Henry Miller with a shrunken head. Dave was wrong, of course. J.C. Curtis was a long way from being an acephalous editor; he had been an editorial writer on the New York *Sun* for fifteen years before it folded. When that great paper died, the way they do sometimes for no apparent reason, our absentee publisher had hired him as Managing Editor, probably the brightest move the publisher had ever made. I don't know why he stayed or why he appeared to be content in Lake Springs, but I don't suppose there was too much difference for the old man between living in a hotel room in New York and living in a hotel room in Florida. Most of his waking hours were spent at the office anyway.

"What do you think personally about this case, Hudson?" J.C. said at last.

"I haven't given it much thought, Mr. Curtis. I was pretty busy, doing a lot of running around out there and all. Just another suicide I suppose."

"There's no such thing as just another suicide. Don't you think there's something peculiar about it?"

"No, sir. There isn't any funny business here. I talked to Riddell, and he said it's definitely murder–suicide, no question about it. Jack Huneker's completely covered—"

"That isn't what I mean, Hudson. I know it's suicide, but why kill two children? Mothers don't usually do this; it's more common with the fathers."

"It happens all the time." I smiled. "And besides, she gave her reason in the note she left. She wanted to be sure her children would get into Heaven before they sinned. So she was evidently a religious fanatic."

"No," J.C. shook his head. "She was a Roman Catholic, and they aren't fanatics."

"They aren't?" I said dubiously. "Not even Father Coughlin?"

"He didn't commit suicide. The Roman Catholic Church doesn't allow suicide. They even have a prohibition on burials, and a lot of after-death malarkey."

"I realize it's unusual," I admitted. "I don't know how much dough Mr. Huneker makes, but he's got a going business with those concrete blocks, especially since they started construction on the retirement village. He's got two cars, a convertible Impala and a Buick station wagon. They've got a beautiful home on the lake, and a private boat dock—"

"Then you'd say the late Mrs. Huneker had everything to live for? A well-to-do husband, two lovely children, and enough money to do practically anything she wanted. Right? And yet, a woman with all this, shoots her children and herself and blames it on TV."

"She had to give some kind of a reason. For suicides, a note of farewell is *de rigueur*, you know. Think of her social position, Mr. Curtis. What would all her friends at the Beachcomber's Club think if she hadn't left a note?"

"I'm concerned about this case, Hudson. Did you know that suicide ranks as the number nine cause of death in the United States?"

I shrugged indifferently. "I think you're taking this too hard, Mr. Curtis. We only lost a reader, not the subscription."

"Now just listen for a minute," J.C. said calmly, not raising his voice. I nodded, and then listened. He *was* the Managing Editor.

"There's an upswing trend in America, Hudson, all across the country. I'm not the first man to notice it, by any means, but the suicide rate has increased gradually ever since 1947. And you can't pass it off due to population increase, either. Contrary to what people believe, there were damned few suicides during the Depression compared to the prosperous days we have now. Sweden, which has always been prosperous, per capita-wise, has always led in world suicide statistics, but we're catching up fast.

"So here's what I want you to do. I want you to dig into the reasons behind Mrs. Huneker's murder–suicide and come up with some valid answers. It'll make a good Sunday feature, and perhaps an entire series on suicide."

I laughed ruefully. "When do I do all this? On your time or mine?"

"You know damned well this isn't a Guild shop; I can't give you any overtime. But if you write something we can use, I'll see that you get some extra money out of it. And I don't mean space rates."

I shook my head. "It's a waste of time, Mr. Curtis. I don't object to digging around for dirt or scandal, if there is any, but all I could possibly find out is external information. The only person who could tell me why is Mrs. Huneker, and she's dead.

"In fiction, I could make up all of her thoughts before suicide and come up with a plausible, readable solution, but this is the real thing. The facts of life are these: birth, living, and death. Our birth, we don't remember. Death? We never know when or how it's going to happen and we don't even think about it because it's all a little frightening. The living process, yours,

mine, or Mrs. Huneker's, is meaningless. What good would it
do for me to find out what kind of toothpaste she used? Or
what she did for amusement? Her life wouldn't differ by a hair,
except for her religion maybe, from any one of those useless
women in her same social bracket.

"And suppose I did learn something scandalous? A lover, for
instance, who threw her over. You couldn't print it because Mr.
Jack Huneker is an advertiser. The police say the case is closed,
and I'm not interested."

"I don't care whether you're interested or not. It's your
assignment."

"Why not give it to Dibs Allen?"

"A sports writer? You know what I think of sports writers."

"What about Dave Finney then? He's the journalism graduate
around here. He'd eat something like this up, for Christ's sake."

"I'll put it another way. Do you like your job, Hudson?" J.C.
snapped the question, and I didn't like the way he said it. To my
disgust my palms began to sweat.

"Sure. Sure I do, Mr. Curtis," I said quickly, hating myself
for saying it. But the way he was staring at me made me realize
that I was an employee, not a permanent fixture around the
newspaper office.

"So you aren't interested, you say." J.C. drummed on the
glass top of his desk, and looked reflectively at the ceiling. "I
never thought I'd hear you say that, Hudson. Five years ago
you entered this office, a raw youth, and asked me for a job—"

"Yeah. A Raw Youth, by Fyodor Dostoevsky. I was twenty-
five, a married man and a father, a college graduate, and I had
finished two years in the Army."

"I know. A raw youth. 'I'm a playwright,' you said, 'not a
journalism student, but before I can write plays, Mr. Curtis, I
have to know all about people.'"

"Did I say that?" I grinned, and felt my face grow warm. "It sounds pretty juvenile."

"You said that, Hudson, and very convincingly, too. So I hired you. Six months later you were doing an adequate job of reporting. So-so, nothing more. And now, five years later, you're still doing an adequate job. Careless, but a typical example of a small-town reporter. Good enough—and I don't expect to find any better ones in a town this size—for a newspaper with an advertising monopoly."

"I don't have that coming, Mr. Curtis," I said self-righteously. "I'm always on time, and I turn in as much copy as anyone else. More than most of the people around here, and—"

"Simmer down, boy." A fleeting smile cracked the M.E.'s lips. "I'm not going to fire you."

"I don't give a damn if you do!" I lied. "If a man can't discuss a story with the editor without being threatened, I don't want to work here!"

"I didn't threaten you, boy, or at least I didn't mean to. But lately I've been worried about you, that's all," he added gently.

"I don't see why." His new tone bewildered me. "I really like my job, Mr. Curtis. And if I've fallen into slovenly habits I'll do my best to correct them."

"A little carelessness doesn't bother me, Hudson. We've got a copy desk to catch mistakes, and a good proofreader downstairs. If there ever was such a thing as good news-writing, there isn't anymore, and I don't expect to unearth any talent in Lake Springs. But I am concerned about your lack of interest in people. This is new with you, and maybe you don't realize it. And another thing. You've been on the night shift for three years. Not once in that time have you bitched about it or asked for a transfer to the *Evening Press*."

"I just happen to prefer the morning sheet, that's all. If a man likes what he's doing, why should he complain about it?"

"What about your wife? Does she like it, too? Not having you at home, six nights a week?"

"At first she didn't like it, but Beryl's used to it now."

"How old is your boy?"

"Eight, almost nine."

"When do you see him?"

"I see him every day. He gets home from school about the time I leave for work, and while he changes into his play clothes we generally shoot the breeze for a while. And then, I see him all day on Sunday."

"Do you consider this a satisfactory, normal father–son relationship?"

"Now look, Mr. Curtis," I said ill-humoredly, "let's leave my wife and child out of this discussion. I don't want to work days. I prefer to work at night. If you're trying to talk me into trading places with Dave Finney, you're wasting your time. I've got everything running the way I want it, a nice little schedule going, and I don't want any changes. If you want to transfer me arbitrarily, that's your privilege as the M.E. But if you do I'll irritate you every day until you change me back."

"The only way you'll ever get on the day shift, Hudson," J.C. slapped his desk, "is to ask for it!"

Rubbing my damp palms on my knees, I sat back in the chair. J.C. rummaged in the center drawer of his desk, and withdrew some ragged yellow sheets of AP wire copy. "This is some stuff I've been saving for several weeks, Hudson, and it'll be of some use to you on your articles. Listen to this," and he read from the copy, "'Suicide, with from 16,000 to 18,000 annual fatalities in the United States, claims more lives than such conditions as diabetes, muscular dystrophy, multiple sclerosis, and infantile paralysis combined.

"'In addition, the problems, costs, and sorrows surrounding both the successful and the much larger number of unsuccessful attempts make the impact of the overall aspects of suicide a major national problem.' I've got a lot of stuff like that saved." J.C. passed me the copy, which I reluctantly accepted.

I whistled softly. "Sixteen to eighteen thousand a year, huh? I didn't know the rate was that high. It's probably a result of all those soldiers stationed in Japan since 1947. In addition to bringing back social diseases, they brought back social customs."

"The U.S. suicide rate is higher than Japan's," J.C. snapped. "Do you still think it's unimportant?"

"I don't think at all, Mr. Curtis. I'm a reporter, not an analyst. You want me to write a series on suicide so that's what I'll do. Okay? Can I go now?"

"Yes, you can go. But the way you've been building up that hard shell of cynicism around you lately—it wouldn't surprise me if you were the next one to go."

From the doorway I smiled and shook my head. "You know something, Mr. Curtis? That prescient mind of yours is beginning to crack. You're working too hard. Why don't you take a long vacation, or better yet, a sabbatical year in Newfoundland where you can cool your feverish brain? Twelve and fourteen hours down here every day is beginning to affect your judgment."

Back at my desk I printed SUICIDE SERIES across the face of a large manila envelope, and stuffed the copy J.C. had given me inside. As an afterthought I scribbled another line on the envelope before putting it away in the bottom drawer. *"Mine, Dave. Don't touch. R.H."* This would be another R.H. factor for Dave's intellectual mind to ponder when he ran across the envelope on the morrow.

There were several notes for fillers on my pad, but it was after midnight and the deadline had come and gone. Of course,

I could have written them anyway to turn in the next night, but I didn't feel like writing anything. A suicide series in particular.

The M.E.'s attitude had shaken me a little, but I was also filled with the remembrance of what I had seen at the Huneker house earlier in the evening. I didn't really know whether I had come close to being fired, or whether J.C. was merely riding me. With a man like that, it was almost impossible to fathom whether he was serious or not. In a lot of ways, I'd be better off if I was canned from the lousy job.

After five years I still made only seventy-five unsanforized bucks a week, which was about as high as I could go as a staff writer. The prospects for a raise of any kind were hopeless— it was that kind of a newspaper. The *Morning News*, *Evening Press*, and the joint *Sunday News-Press* were part of a chain of forty Southern newspapers. The high cost of newsprint had frozen the daily combined circulation to thirty thousand copies. If the publisher bought additional newsprint to increase the circulation another ten thousand daily copies—which could be accomplished easily—the charges for all his paper would be raised correspondingly, and in the long run he would make less money than he was making from the *News-Press* now. The theory, of course, was that he could jack up his advertising rates to offset the costs. Unfortunately, the *News-Press* had enjoyed a monopoly for so many years already, the advertising rates had been jacked up so high that the local advertisers couldn't afford any new jump in rates. In fact, they considered the current rates exorbitant, which they were, and to advertise in the *Morning News* they were forced to take a similar ad in the *Evening Press* whether they wanted it or not. Stalemate.

On a hot local story, the Marion Huneker murder–suicide for instance, the *Morning News* streetsale copies would be sold out before 10:00 A.M. A resident of Lake Springs, or of one of the surrounding smaller towns, who wanted to keep up with the sales and supermarket specials, was forced to subscribe to both the morning and evening papers. He couldn't take one or the other. The news delivery boys wouldn't accept a subscription for just one paper at only fifty cents a week. And the circulation manager had to accept this rule of the newsboys in order to get competent boys to deliver the papers. Even with two daily papers, if the subscribers wanted good news coverage they had to take one of the Miami sheets.

The local news was fairly sketchy. We relied mostly on syndicated features and columnists to fill the spaces above the advertisements, but the two wire services furnished enough world and national news to keep our subscribers from belly-aching too loudly. The publisher of the chain had a standard formula for all of his papers. It worked. He made money. Why should he fool around with it?

At loose ends I got up from my desk and wandered over to the window. The downtown streets had been rolled up and put away. At the four-way stop on the corner, the lights had been turned to all yellow, and they blinked away at only occasional motorists.

That little boy, Antonio, 8, the same age as my own son, was dead; dead before he had ever had a chance to find out for himself what a rotten world he lived in. It wasn't fair. Seeing the little girl, Kathy, hadn't been so bad. But like a damned fool, I had followed Riddell up the tree and into the treehouse to take a look at the dead boy. The Huneker kid had been chubby, and he had been doubled up in one corner of the tiny treehouse, both fat hands clasped to his little round belly where his mother had shot him. What a dirty, self-pitying bitch!

And the pitiful little girl, trying to hide beneath her bed! Six years old, a baby! She had probably hidden under her bed, in play, from her brother, a dozen times or more, and considered it a nice, safe hiding place...

These were two good reasons why I didn't want to write an article about Mrs. Huneker; I detested the woman. I had never met her, and I didn't know her problems, and even if I had known her I wouldn't have lifted a finger to prevent her from killing herself. To end one's own life is a privilege under the U.S. Constitution, in my opinion, and if a person's pursuit of happiness lies in that direction, the person should be encouraged to follow it, by all means.

But for a mother to murder her two, innocent, little children, and kill them painfully at that, using the Gates of Heaven as an excuse...! I tried to think of something worse, and as usual, I succeeded. Marion Huneker, at least, had completed the job she started. Although I begrudged it, I had to give her that much credit.

About two years before, I had accompanied two cops to the retirement village on an investigation concerning a shot that had been fired. We found an old man of eighty in his small, pink house, crying hysterically, and cradling his dead wife's bloody head in his lap. The old couple had made a suicide pact, and he had shot his wife first. Then it was his turn, and the old man was unable to pull the trigger. All he could do, after we arrived on the scene, was to weep and beg the police officers to kill him. To top this off, he had been suffering from an incurable cancer. He had died in the city hospital, less than a month later, and was never brought to trial.

Yes. That was worse.

No. Not much worse.

Under the circumstances I couldn't allow myself to remain prejudiced against the late Mrs. Huneker. To investigate her death I had to be objective. As the old master, Ben Hecht, said: "To show emotion, be callous."

I sat down at my desk again and wrote a note to Dave Finney suggesting a visit to Huneker's neighbors in the morning to get a feature story for the *Evening News*. I weighted the note in the center of the desk with a brass ruler, and slipped into my jacket.

Without waiting for the press run, to get a copy of the morning paper to check out my story, I left the office and drove home. I was tired; dead tired.

Chapter Two

I fought my way out of a sound sleep, sluggishly and persistently, at precisely 10:30 A.M. the next morning. I always awakened at 10:30, and at least 300 days out of 365, I awoke dripping with perspiration, due to the hot, humid Florida climate. My pillow was wet and stained with sweat, but my wife didn't change slips until Saturday, and this was only Tuesday.

The unvaried unconscious routine: a session in the john, a shave, followed by a heart-shaped dexedrine tablet, swallowed hastily with tepid water from a toothbrush glass, to dispel the confusion of sleep and to prime my sodden brain for thinking. Then a cup of muddy coffee, maybe two, sometimes three.

The coffee was truly foul. Always.

My wife was always up before seven to prepare breakfast for Buddy and to get him off to school. Beryl rarely drank more than one cup of coffee (and she used a sugar substitute called *Sweetums* to preserve her figure). The early brew, boiled at seven, sat on the warm electric burner until I got out of bed. By 10:45 or 11:00, when I poured this dark liquid into my cup, a chemical metamorphosis of some kind transformed the coffee into a pitchblack species of slimy mud. After two cupfuls, however, I was as bright-eyed as a puppy—but maybe the dexedrine had something to do with it.

"I'm ready for my breakfast, Beryl!" I called peremptorily through the glass jalousies of the back door to my wife. She was hanging laundry on the clothesline in the back yard, and although she said something in reply, I couldn't understand her because her mouth was full of clothespins.

To my third cup of coffee, I added three spoonfuls of sugar, and kept adding homogenized milk until the liquid turned to a lovely shade of flophouse wallpaper gray.

Still in my pajama trousers I stumbled around the living room gathering scattered sheets of the *Morning News*. Buddy read the comic sections faithfully at breakfast, but to find them, he found it necessary to take the newspaper completely apart every morning. When I first started work I used to bring a free paper home every day, but after I forgot to do so a few times, my wife had taken out a subscription. Buddy could be trying when he missed the daily comic strips.

My story was on the right half of the front page, and it read much better in print than it had in typescript. There was also a two-column photo of the late Mrs. Huneker accompanying the story. The smile on her lovely face was so wide her lower teeth were exposed as much as her uppers. She was wearing an old-fashioned cloche hat, which was decorated with arabesques of silvery embroidery. There was a double-strand of large pearls dangling to her waist. The sack dress, cut low in front, revealed an indecent amount of breast cleavage. She was an attractive woman all right, but for a moment I was puzzled by her choice of attire. Then I remembered. The photograph had been on file in the negative morgue, and she was wearing the costume she had worn in the Beachcomber's Follies two years ago. The theme of that particular annual charity amateur show had been The Gay 'Twenties, and she had taken a role of some kind.

Chuck Russell, the staff photographer, had also made a feeble effort at a human interest photo. A two-column cut, below the flip end of my story, presented a stuffed panda bear and a toy wagon on the Huneker's front porch to catch the morbid reader's attention. The overline above the photo asked plaintively in

10-point boldface: "Who Will Play With Us Now?" That was the deft hand of Harris, no doubt of it.

Beryl came into the kitchen from the back yard, closed the door with her hip, and tossed an empty cardboard box into the utility room. She began to prepare my breakfast.

"Did you read my story about the suicide?"

"I heard about it on TV," she replied. "It was on the eleven-fifteen news."

"That's loyalty for you," I muttered, and turned apathetically to Drew Pearson.

Except for two army years at Camp Hood, Texas, I've eaten the same breakfast every morning since I was eight years old: two fried eggs, two pieces of crisp bacon, grits and melted butter, and two slices of toast. As Beryl set the plate before me, she spoke again, this time with the familiar, ingratiating, favor-seeking tone of voice. "There are a couple of things I'd like to have you do for me this morning, honey—"

"What now?" I said sourly, poking the yolks with a fork.

"Just little things, but I can't get to all of them by myself. There're two more loads of wash this morning, and you'll have to go to the store for me. The list is already made out, and Tide is on sale today. Then if you'll pick up the dry cleaning and Buddy's shoes at the repair shop, I'll be through here in time to take the car down for an oil change. I looked at the little sticker on the door yesterday, and it's been more than two thousand miles since the oil was changed."

"To you," I said bitterly, "these are just little things, but every damned day it's some *little* thing! And that's exactly why my play isn't finished. I've told you a hundred times, but you can't seem to get it into your thick skull—the only reason I took the night shift was to have free time during the day to work on my play."

"All right. Never mind. I'll get to everything. Somehow. You go ahead and work on your play."

"I don't want to be unreasonable," I relented. "I know you've got a lot to do. But every single day you manage to involve me in some sort of domestic entanglement. I'll pick up the shoes and dry cleaning for you, but you can do the shopping later. And the car can go a few more miles without changing the oil. We only drive it around town anyway."

"Never mind. Forget it."

The washing machine was right across the room from my chair. Beryl started to load it from the huge pile of laundry on the floor. The smell of these dirty clothes didn't help my appetite in the slightest way. She poured a measure of soap powder on top of the clothes, slammed the lid, and pushed one green button and two red buttons. A noise came up like thunder.

"I'll go to the store now," Beryl said, raising her voice above the noise of the machine. "You can listen to the laundry from your study. If it starts to go bumpety, bumpety, bump, hurry in and turn it off."

"What's the matter with it?"

"It's the agitator, I think."

"Well, you'd better take care of it. We can't afford a new one."

"On your salary we can't afford a new anything."

A crack like that could really set me off, but this time I let it pass. A single man has bacon and eggs for breakfast; a married man has an argument. Beryl left the kitchen, went into the bedroom, and emerged a couple of minutes later with her purse and a new red mouth.

"You aren't going to the store like that?" I said.

"I am," she replied calmly, groping through her straw handbag for her keys to the Chevy. "It's eighty degrees today."

Beryl was wearing blue cotton short shorts, and a blue-and-white bandana halter. Her long straight legs were tanned evenly, and her ample breasts strained against the halter; the girl took damned good care of herself. She was a pleasure to look at, in fact to stare at...

If not the dumbest, Beryl had been the prettiest freshman at the University. And the day she flunked out I felt as if I should drink the tears that washed her pretty face—as my penance. It had been my fault she flunked out, not hers. Through constant practice, I had developed an ability to cram hard for an hour or so before an exam and pass it with comparative ease. Of course, I retained little or nothing about the subject a week later, but knowledge was irrelevant; the main idea was to pass the exam at hand. A man should never let education interfere with the obtaining of his degree. Without a diploma, what is knowledge?

But Beryl needed no diploma for her beauty. No man can describe his wife accurately. He is bound to be prejudiced one way or the other, and besides, he knows all of her faults too damned well.

By any standards of beauty, Beryl certainly wasn't plain, but perhaps she wasn't gorgeous, either. Scott Fitzgerald wrote a descriptive passage for one of his feminine characters that almost fitted Beryl exactly: "She was a faded but still beautiful woman of twenty-seven." And Beryl was now twenty-seven. Sometimes she looked about twenty-three, as I remembered her at twenty-three, but there were days when she looked much closer to thirty, trying to pass herself off as twenty-seven. She had long, black hair (I didn't allow her to cut it), and cerium gray eyes that turned into cobalt blue the moment she stepped outside and the sun fell on her face. She was too old to wear her long hair in a ponytail, confined by a rubber band, but she wore it that way most of the time anyway, out of defiance to me,

I supposed, because I refused to let her chop it off. But this morning, all of a sudden, she looked very young and incredibly desirable.

"Well," I said grimly, "I'm not going to order you not to wear short shorts, but if you get raped someday, don't say I didn't warn you."

"That would be better than nothing." She smiled sweetly, and fluttered her long lashes.

"What's that supposed to mean?"

"You know exactly what I mean."

I cleared my throat. "It's not my fault. You told me you were off the roof. What do you expect me to do?"

"That was ten days ago."

"That long?" I was truly astonished.

"That long." She opened the front door.

"Wait!" I crossed the room hurriedly, closed the door, and put my back to it. I grinned. "Far be it from me to deny my wife a sexual favor. And there will never be a better time than now." I reached out toward her, and she stepped back.

"No," she snapped. "I'm going to the store."

"You can go to the store afterwards."

"Go to hell, Richard Hudson! You'll never see the day when I'll agree to hinting around for one of your sexual *favors*!"

"I didn't mean anything," I said smoothly, moving toward her slowly.

"I mean it," she said threateningly. "And you can go straight to hell!" Her voice was so serious I had to laugh. But she cut off my laughter by swinging her weighted straw bag by its carrying strap; it was so unexpected I didn't have time to duck, and the leather bottom of the bag raked across my face. I wasn't hurt, although my face stung slightly, but the expression on my face must have frightened her.

"I told you to let me alone," she said, half-apologetically.

But by then I was close enough to grab her. I jerked the straw bag out of her hand and tossed it on the couch, and heaved her body over my shoulder. She pounded her fists on my back as I carried her into the bedroom. I dumped her onto the bed, and closed the bedroom door.

"I said now," I reminded her.

"And I said no!" she replied.

I shrugged, but it was with an indifference I didn't really feel. The idea that she had put up a little resistance, as ineffectual as it had been, had added a certain element of excitement to an event that was ordinarily a rather routine affair.

"Okay, sweetie, if that's the way you want it." I grinned. "I told you you'd get raped one of these days if you wore those short shorts—but I didn't think it would be me. Take 'em off!"

"No!" She was really angry now. Her face was flushed, and her eyes glared at me through a moist shine of rage.

I ripped them off; the big white button on the left side whizzed across the room as I easily tore the cotton material. I flipped her over—she didn't resist—and unfastened the halter. I rolled her on her back again, and tossed the halter onto the dresser. Her limpness, her silence, made me apprehensive. "Do I have to rip off the panties, too?" I asked.

There was no reply. She sighed wearily, and stared at the ceiling. I rolled the panties down carefully over her hips, and pulled them from under her buttocks. I got them off, somehow, without tearing them. Her breasts were heaving, and I thought she was going to give me the passive, suffering treatment—just lie there motionless and let me go through the motions. The martyr bit. I was ready now to say the hell with it, but I was as stubborn as she was. I undressed, and the moment my knee touched the bed, she rolled over toward the wall like an otter twisting under water. I went after her, scrambling, not caring now whether I hurt her or not. I caught her by the waist with both hands, and pulled her toward me hard, with a half-crazed desire filling me with lust. I was determined to make her submit to me.

Suddenly she giggled, twisting sideways, and her hip was between my legs. Again and again I tried to pin her flat, but she twisted and turned, or jerked her knees up hard. Twice she managed to get me right in the pit of the stomach with one of her sharp knees before I finally forced my right leg between her thighs. But it didn't help me any; she simply locked her legs tightly around my trembling leg so I couldn't move it. Breathing hard, I tried to relax for a moment, and she bit me on the chest. She raked my back with her sharp nails before I could catch her wrists. Desperate, I held both of her wrists with my left hand, and reached down to where she was vulnerable, gripping her soft thighs hard with my fingers, prying them open brutally. She cried out then, first angrily, and then in pain, sinking her sharp teeth into my shoulder so ferociously that the skin ripped. I could feel and hear it rip—and then her hot tongue lapped at the burning spot on my shoulder and I realized she was licking my blood. I was frantic, frenzied, and forced my way inside. She met me all the way, arching her back, writhing, demanding, mewing deep in her throat until I was spent completely. I rolled to one side, without any strength left at all.

Not Beryl. She bounced up cheerfully, in a hurry to beat me to the bathroom, as fresh as a May morning.

"Now, that's more like it!" she said happily, and a moment later she was singing under the shower.

After the car pulled out of the driveway, I dropped the Venetian blinds in the living room and switched on the television set. I was going to have to make up a sex schedule of some kind—

only ten days had gone by, but suppose I had let the whole month pass by? My shoulder was still sore, and burning under the bandaid. But in a way, I was grateful for the way things had worked out. After nine years of marriage, something like that was needed once in a while to break up the routine sameness a married sexual relationship drifts into....

The sound blasted away on the set, drowning the rumble of the thundering washing machine in the kitchen, and I turned my attention to the screen. A cowboy, with a rope around his neck, stood on the flat bed of a wagon. There was a fair-sized crowd around the wagon, screaming and yelling. A burly, bearded individual whipped the two horses attached to the wagon and they galloped forward. The man was left hanging by the neck from the limb of the cottonwood tree. Two shots were fired, the rope parted, and the hanging man fell to the ground. The crowd fled, scattering, looking apprehensively over their shoulders, and disappeared from the scene. A cowboy appeared, dressed completely in black, riding a white horse. He holstered his smoking pistol, dismounted, and kneeled beside the man on the ground. The man on the ground sat up and rubbed his sore neck gingerly with the tips of his fingers.

"That's a mighty nasty rope burn you got there, pardner," the black-clad rescuer remarked sympathetically. "What you need is Riche's Oil! Good for *all* types of burns!" He reached inside his black shirt and pulled out a bottle of Riche's Oil.

All during the subsequent selling spiel, concerning the virtues of Riche's Oil, the rescued cowboy kept reaching for the oil, but the rescuer held it away from him, claiming additional uses for the product.

No comment. I turned off the set, raised the Venetian blinds, and went into my study. I closed and locked the door, sat down at my battered desk inherited from my father. Every man needs a place to go, a place where he won't be bothered by anybody. The study was my place.

There were a couple of hundred books—all plays—in the unpainted, floor-to-ceiling, built-in bookcase. But I kept the one-volume edition of Shakespeare's complete plays, along with a dictionary and a thesaurus, on my desk at all times. From a blurb on the front cover of a John D. MacDonald paperback, I had clipped a quotation and scotchtaped it across the face of my Shakespeare:

"I wish I had written this book!"
                                        Mickey Spillane

This had seemed funny at the time I did it, but it was funny no longer. The unfinished manuscript of the play I had been working on for three years mocked me every day. After three years of almost daily work, I had completed only thirty-five pages. And yet I stuck with it, because there was only one way I could escape my current plight and job in Lake Springs: write and have produced a successful Broadway play. In addition to becoming rich from my play, I also wanted fame. An idle dream? Perhaps. But this was my dream, and I was stuck with it for lack of a better one.

The theme of the play was quite simple, like all great plays, but it was also intricately complicated because of all the thought and time I had put into it every day. The thirty-five complete pages were written in blank verse. A dozen earlier versions of the play had been written and destroyed before I had decided to write the play in verse form.

Briefly, very briefly, my play, which I had entitled *The Understudy*, was four little plays within the framework of a larger play. The plot, quite simply, concerned a gifted amateur actor, who was employed as a dishwasher. During a season of community theater plays, the dishwasher–actor conspired and plotted to steal the job of the well-educated community theater director. He did this by aping the mannerisms and skills of the director and in the end succeeded in his plans. The final lines before the last act curtain were these:

DIRECTOR
(Bewilderedly) Why, why did you do this to me?

DISHWASHER
Incentive, O disposed one.
A dishwasher has no future.
But if you, too, require incentive
To equal my hard-earned success —
I know where a dishwashing job is open…
                    (Final Curtain)

After three years, however, this idea, which had seemed fresh and original in the beginning, now seemed trite and dull, which, perhaps it had been all along. Starting over in blank verse had given me new inspiration, and the deeper meanings, shades, and nuances of thought that had been beyond my grasp in straight prose and dialogue, were beginning to fall murkily into place. The nebulous verse images I sweated over appeared to put across the essential meanings I didn't quite understand myself.

In an autobiographical way, I was both director and dishwasher, player and understudy. I had majored in speech and theater arts at college, although I had never staged a play. I had always aspired to writing plays, not acting or directing, and had received straight A's in college playwriting classes. Three of my one-act plays had been produced by student–actors, and my best one-acter, *The Senile Delinquent*, had won the Mrs. Cora Lowey Averell Award—a check for $100 and a college production.

Bolstered, if not inflated, by these schoolboy successes, I

had expected to have at least one play running on Broadway within a year after graduation. But as a married man and a father, I had been forced to get a job of some kind, and because my father had left me his house in Lake Springs when he died, I had gone home again, taking Beryl and Buddy with me.

My father had been a retired Lake Springs policeman, a sergeant in charge of the Traffic Division, and well known around town. If the *News-Press* hadn't hired me, I would have found something else to do easily enough. The old man had been the responsible type, and I had tried to live up to his example. My mother had divorced him when I was only nine years old, and had moved back to New Jersey. But when Dad died I had written her a letter telling her that she was welcome to come and live with Beryl and me if she so desired. The letter had not been acknowledged, but I had considered this the right thing to do, and I had felt quite self-satisfied with myself for a few days for making the attempt.

In addition to having the qualifications of the Director in my play, my dead-end job on the *News-Press* gave me equal billing with the Dishwasher. Certainly no would-be playwright had greater incentive than I to escape from a miserable situation and to gain success in his chosen field. I considered news-writing not only a poor form of writing, but a ridiculous type of writing—dull, factual, prosaic, transitory, ritualistic, formulaized, and unrewarding in every respect.

At twenty-five I had deliberately gone after the reporting job because of the incentive it would give me to write my first play—but somewhere along the line something had gone wrong. Now I was thirty, and I hadn't written my play yet, I was in a deep but comfortable rut, and it was rather pleasant. I no longer detested my job; in many ways I rather enjoyed it, working at night in particular.

Why? Who? When? Where? What? And sometimes How? These were a newspaperman's questions, not a playwright's.

In sudden disgust with myself I ripped the pages of my first act in half. I was immediately remorseful, and carefully put the torn sheets away in the middle drawer of the desk. Too many hours, too much thought and effort had gone into that first act to destroy it and start over again. Feeling miserable and filled with self-pity, I left the study, showered, and got dressed to go downtown. I was trying to decide on a necktie when Beryl drove the old Chevy under the carport.

"Where are you going?" she said sharply, putting the bag of groceries she was carrying down on the dinette table.

I was planning to attend a movie, but it would have been ill-advised to admit this to my wife. "The M.E. has given me a special assignment," I said, knotting my tie. "He wants me to write some sort of series for the Sunday Feature Section."

"You can't work night and day too."

"This assignment will mean some extra dough if the pieces turn out all right."

"Can the newspaper spare it?"

"I think so. That's what I'm going to talk to Mr. Curtis about now. Oh. And I'll have the car greased and the oil changed while I'm downtown."

Beryl followed me to the door, slipped her arm about my waist. She kissed me goodbye, a long wet one. Her breath was bad, sulphurous from the hard-boiled eggs she had eaten for breakfast. "Wake me," she said self-consciously, "when you get home tonight. If you aren't too tired."

"Sure. You bet." I opened the door.

"And will you bring the garbage can in before you go?"

"The garbage can?"

"This is Tuesday," Beryl explained patiently, for perhaps the thousandth time. "Every Tuesday and Friday morning the garbage is picked up. If I can carry the full can out to the curb before I go to bed, it seems like the least you can do is bring the empty can back around—"

"Why can't Buddy bring it around when he gets home from school?"

"Because I need the can to put garbage in. Now!"

"Sure."

I got the can, put the lid on, and carried it through the back gate to the concrete platform beside the kitchen door. Before Beryl could trap me into doing any more domestic chores I ran desperately for the Chevy in the carport and backed into the street.

Downtown, I left the car at Bunny's Garage and asked the mechanic to park it in the newspaper parking lot (a block down the street) when he completed the grease job. I got to the Sunshine Theater at 12:50, right after the doors had opened, beating the one o'clock price change. As usual, the old ticket-taker shook hands with me, and tried to give me a synopsis of the movie I was about to see. But I managed to get away from him before he finished, not that it makes any difference; all movies end the same way. The important thing about attending a movie in Florida is the state of the theater's air-conditioning system, and the Sunshine Theater was always cool.

At three-thirty I emerged again, blinking into the sun. There was time enough for a sandwich and a Coca-Cola before I was due at the office.

"Ah, yes!" I thought with grisly satisfaction. "The newspaper!" Without my wonderful job, my life would be the most monotonous and boring existence in the entire world.

It Just Don't Make Sense!

By Dave Finney

News–Press Staff Writer

"It just don't make sense!" Mrs. Gertrude S. Slater, 1410 Lake Shore Drive, told this reporter, with reference to the suicide of Mrs. Marion C. Huneker, her neighbor, who fatally shot her two children before taking her own life last night.

"I've known Marion (Mrs. Huneker) ever since she and her husband moved down here from Pittsburgh," Mrs. Slater continued, "and I never knew a woman more interested in life than she was.

"Only last week she asked me for a cutting off my flame vine, said she wanted to train it up the poles along her carport. That's what I mean. That don't sound like any woman planning to kill herself, does it? It just don't make sense!"

Mr. Thomas Fessier, longtime employee for the Magic Garden Spray & Lawn Maintenance Service, had this to say: "I've been taking care of the Hunekers' lawn for more than two years now. Mrs. Huneker was always fussy about her lawn, not that she was unreasonable or anything like a lot of people, but she liked things just so.

"Last Tuesday, it was, when I mowed her lawn, I told her it needed spraying again. The chinch bugs were beginning to get a nice bite out in back, you see. We must have talked for a good half-hour or more; she was asking about replanting with dichondra. A woman planning a complicated project like that, which would take a lot of work to get started, it just don't figure she's going to shoot her kids and herself. When I read about it in the paper this morning I could hardly believe it."

Another friend and neighbor of Mrs. Huneker's, Mrs. Lawrence B. McKeldin, 1402 Lake Shore Drive, had known the deceased three years, as a member of the Wednesday Afternoon Bridge Club.

"This wasn't any tightly organized club," Mrs. McKeldin explained. "It was more of an informal get-together of four girls, so to speak. But Marion (Mrs. Huneker) was definitely one of the group.

"We met almost every Wednesday afternoon, taking turns at each other's homes. We play Culbertson, and most people today have switched to Goren. What I'm getting to is this:

"Only two or three weeks ago, I had a long talk with Marion about Jacoby. She wanted us to get a book on Jacoby and plan a full afternoon where we could discuss his system of play. It was all I could do to dissuade her from this idea. But she was very cheerful, not disappointed about it. Marion was an animated person, with a keen interest in bridge, and although she liked to win, like every good player, she was philosophical when she lost. All of the girls in the club were shocked by the news, and we're sending a wreath..."

Several neighbors and friends of Mrs. Huneker this reporter interviewed requested that they not be quoted, although none of them could advance a reason for the double-murder and suicide.

The late Mrs. Huneker's priest, Fr. Donald Hardy, SJ, pastor of The Church of the Sacred Heart, and Dr. Maxwell Goldman, the Huneker's family doctor, had "no comment" concerning the deceased matron.

Chapter Three

Dave's story, beneath a 42 point Ludlow Coronet head, took up two parallel columns on the left side of the front page in the *Evening Press*. There were half-column cuts of Mrs. Slater, Mr. Fessier, and Mrs. McKeldin set into the copy opposite their banal remarks. I dropped the paper flat on the desk, clasped my hands behind my head, and grinned fondly at Dave Finney.

Dave had been a journalism major at the University of Miami, and actually considered journalism as a "profession." His dark sienna eyes were alert and inquisitive, and he wore his hair in a brush cut. No matter how hot it was—even in the middle of summer—he wore a coat and tie to add dignity to his profession. He was only twenty-four, and planned to get a good "grounding" on a small city newspaper before becoming a foreign correspondent. An eager type. We usually talked to each other every day for a few minutes before I took over the desk.

"What do you think of it, Richard?" Dave said anxiously, meaning his by-lined story, not the murder–suicide.

"It just do not make sense," I replied, shaking my head sadly.

Dave blushed slightly. "I was a little worried about that myself," he admitted. "I started to change 'don't' to 'doesn't' and then I thought it sounded more like real dialogue. Besides, that's what she said. I didn't think Mr. Gladden would pick it up for the head, though."

"It just do not make sense," I repeated, with an air of feigned bewilderment.

"Otherwise the story's all right, isn't it?"

"Don't ask me. You're the journalism major around here."

"Well, I didn't sneak the story in." Dave cleared his throat. "Mr. Gladden okayed it," he added defensively, "and he *is* the City Editor."

"You're worried, I take it, because Mr. Curtis didn't get a look at the copy first. Well, Dave," I nodded soberly, "you're wise to worry. Last night J.C. racked me up and down about my first-hand exposition of the case."

"He did? I thought your story was great—"

"You should've seen it before J.C.'s pencil. But I wouldn't worry too much, Dave. J.C. told me that he didn't expect to see good newswriting anymore. So you haven't disappointed him."

"What is wrong with it, then?"

"It just do not make sense," I said again, tasting the words slowly, as if they were sweet. "You haven't told me anything," I continued, seriously. "Now that I've read your story, and I read it twice, what have I learned? Mrs. Huneker was fond of flame vines, she played a fair game of bridge, she had her lawn mowed regularly, and a woman named—" here I had to glance at the story again "—Mrs. McKeldin considered her 'one of the group.' Her priest and doctor, who may have been able to throw a little light on the case, are both down as 'no comment.' Except for these mild criticisms, I'd say it's a fine story. Yes, siree!"

Dave laughed. "What's got into you? You left me the note to interview the neighbors, and Gladden hadn't thought of it. I told him it was my idea, and he considered it a good follow-up, and sent the photographer along. What did you expect me to get, anyway?"

"Nothing. Not really. You got about as much as I would, Dave. You covered a lot of territory in the time you had." I snipped Dave's story out of the paper, pulled out my SUICIDE SERIES envelope, and dropped the clipping inside.

"I just happened to notice that envelope this morning," Dave said, trying to appear unconcerned. "What—"

"J.C. Curtis. The Yankee mind of the M.E. came up with an idea about a suicide series, and gave me the assignment to write it. All I have to do is find out why Mrs. Huneker, a Roman Catholic of Italian parentage, married to a—what is Huneker, anyway? German, Jewish?"

"Beats me," Dave shrugged.

"Anyway, as the colorful oldtime reporters used to put it so colorfully, I'm supposed to find out why she took the Dutch Route."

Dave whistled, and then laughed happily. "What does he expect you to find? I know you think my story's lousy, but—"

"I was only kidding you, Dave."

"All right. But I had to hustle to get as much copy as I did. All of the opinions I got from her neighbors were useless. Dr. Goldman wouldn't tell me anything on the phone, and asked me not to use his name even. There's only one person who can tell you why Mrs. Huneker killed herself, and that's Mrs. Huneker."

"I agree. Now, Mr. Curtis is in his office; I can see him through the glass door. I'd appreciate it if you'd go into his office and tell him his idea smells."

"There might be some interesting angles at that." Dave frowned, plucked thoughtfully at his lower lip.

"Give me one." I snapped my fingers. "Just one."

"I'd have to give it a little thought, and why should I? It's your assignment, not mine." Dave got up from the chair beside the desk and stretched. "I'll look forward to reading your series, Mr. Hudson. I'm a little curious myself about why she killed the children."

"That's easy. All children should be killed at birth. They

make too much noise growing up, and a lot of them end up as journalism majors."

"You're covering the lecture at the Beachcomber's tonight, aren't you?"

"I'd planned on it. Why?"

"Mrs. Huneker was a member. Why don't you see what some of her club members have to say. It's a beginning."

"Thanks for the suggestion," I said dryly. "The thought had occurred to me independently. I believe, if I try hard enough, that I can discover what Mrs. Huneker's favorite drink was, maybe. Yes, yes, you've given me my lead, Dave! 'Mr. Mel Haight, chief bartender at the Beachcomber's Club, stated in an exclusive interview that the late Mrs. Huneker's favorite drink was a tall Tom Collins, on the rocks. It just do not make sense, the bartender continued—'" Dave walked away, shaking his head in disgust, and disappeared down the stairs.

I clipped my own story out of the *Morning News*, added it to the contents of my growing file, and made a few notes. I turned through the phone book, copied Dr. Morris Goldman's clinic address and number into my notebook; but not the priest's address. I knew where Father Hardy lived; he resided in a beautiful, white, two-story house right next to his church, and he had two fulltime servants besides. White servants, at that. Not many Negro Catholics in Lake Springs, I supposed.

Who else? The creative writing teacher, of course. For this information, I checked with Mrs. Mosby, a truly wonderful woman. Mrs. Mosby had been with the *News–Press* forever. Her duties were so varied and numerous, they were almost impossible to sum up coherently. She was the M.E.'s personal secretary, the keeper of the morgue, compiler of the payroll, a writer of classified ads, hand-holder, advice-giver, and a veritable storehouse of information. Her sweet little old gray head held facts and figures about everything and everybody in Lake Springs. The perfect companion to be marooned on an island with, if a man could be that fortunate.

"Mrs. Mosby," I said, "do you happen to know who teaches the so-called creative writing course at the Adult Education Center?"

"Paul Hershey. Monday and Friday evenings, seven-thirty to nine-thirty, Room 103, at the high school."

"That's pretty glib, young lady," I said sternly. "As a rule you have to think for a minute or two."

"Not really, Richard," Mrs. Mosby smiled, and wrinkled her nose. "It just happens that I took Mr. Hershey's course for a while last year."

"How did you find the time?"

"I took the time, but it was time wasted." She shrugged her thin, narrow shoulders. "Oh, not really wasted. A person can always learn something. I wrote two stories, but I've been around the paper too long." She laughed gently. "I crammed my whole story into the first paragraph, instead of holding things back for the end. Fiction's written backward, you know."

"I never looked at it that way, but I suppose you could say fiction was backward. I imagined magazine editors chop their stories off at the first paragraph instead of at the end. How come you dropped out of the class?"

"Well, Mr. Hershey runs a sort of seminar. The class discusses the student's stories after he reads them aloud. It could've been a good course, but there was one old harridan who talked constantly, using the class as a town hall for her own views on everything she could think of. I kept waiting for her to turn in a story of her own so I could get in a few choice critical remarks, but she never did write anything. Too busy talking all the time. I gave up finally, all out of patience."

"What kind of a guy is Mr. Hershey?"

"He's very nice, Richard. Too nice, really. Quite old. He doesn't have a firm control over the class, but he's really a writer, not a teacher."

"Thanks, Mrs. Mosby. Was Mrs. Huneker, by any chance, in your class last year?"

"No, I'm sorry to say. I never met her."

"I'm sorry, too. If you had known her, I could get out of my assignment, and turn it over to you."

"Why I think you're a wonderful reporter, Richard."

"Thank you. You don't know what that remark means to my morale."

I returned to my desk to do a little work. I called the desk sergeant at the police station. Auntie Rosetta had been picked up again for the *nth* time for selling bolita tickets. I had filed too many stories on Auntie Rosetta already, and asked if he had anything else. I had heard the dirty joke he told me, but there was a filler item I could use about a gas station. This was the kind of filler that J.C. liked to see:

Despite the typical October high of 82 degrees yesterday, Winter has arrived at last. Patrick Odium, owner of an independent filling station, 1635 Hotchkiss Rd., reported to the police last night that a northbound motorist had stolen two gallons of Zerex anti-freeze out of his office while he was servicing another car.

As I jerked this hackneyed filler out of the typewriter I saw J.C. Curtis, accompanied by a visitor, approaching my desk, and I got hastily to my feet. The little old man with J.C. was wearing yellow Bermuda shorts and a bright red sport shirt.

"This is Mr. Hudson," J.C. said to the bright-eyed little old man. "This is Mr. Adamski, Hudson. He's celebrating his golden wedding anniversary coming up Sunday. Take care of him." The M.E. turned away and I shook hands with Adamski.

"Sit down, sir," I said cordially. Adamski sat down on the first fourth of the chair beside my desk, and handed me an enormous white leather scrapbook. OUR LIFE was carved into the cover, and the incised letters had been filled in with gold leaf.

"It's all in here, Mr. Hudson," Adamski said eagerly, patting the album with a small arthritic hand. "Fifty wonderful years of a wonderful, wonderful union. Me and Hazel was married fifty years ago come Sunday, and it seems just like only yesterday."

"Well, well. What's your address?"

Adamski gave me his address—he lived in the retirement village—and I wrote it on my pad, along with his age, 76, and his wife's maiden name. Once started, he talked quickly and earnestly; I learned that he was originally from Detroit; that he had been residing in Lake Springs for three years; and that prior to his retirement, he had worked for General Motors as a paint shop sub-foreman.

I leafed idly through the white scrapbook and the old man winked craftily and leaned forward. "Betcha never took me for seventy-six, didja?" he whispered.

"Why no," I replied sharply. "I thought you were in your late eighties."

His face fell and his alert, blue eyes darkened with disappointment. I hadn't intended to be cruel, so I laughed, and clapped him on the shoulder. "I was teasing you, Mr. Adamski. To tell the truth," I lied, "you don't look much more than fifty."

He perked up at once, smiling with self-satisfaction. "I knew you were joking. I never did look my real age. Now that there," he pointed to the open album, "that's a picture of me and Hazel taken in a studio about a year after we was married. Pretty then, wasn't she?"

"You weren't such a bad-looking guy yourself, Pop. That's quite a soup-strainer you were wearing. Were you hiding from the police?"

Adamski cackled delightedly, slapped his bare, bony knee. "No, sir, Mr. Hudson. Everybody was wearing handlebars those days."

"Your wife wasn't."

"I mean the men folks."

"I think we can use this picture. We get a couple of golden anniversary stories every week, and—"

"I know you do. I'm a subscriber. That's how come I came in to see the editor. You ran a big write-up on Mr. Jessup's anniversary, and he's a neighbor of mine. I figured if an old crank like Jessup could get him a write-up, me and Hazel should get one too!"

"When a couple sticks it out for fifty years, Mr. Adamski, the newspaper feels that it's a newsworthy item. But when we can, we like to get a new angle. This old photo is still in good condition, and should reproduce well, so my idea is this: We'll have one of our photographers take a new photo of you and Mrs. Adamski, and then we can run both pictures side by side. What do you think?"

"You can't do it, Mr. Hudson." The old man soberly shook his head.

"Why not? We won't damage your old photo. I'll guarantee it."

"Oh, I'm not worried about that old picture," he waved his hand back and forth in dismissal. "But my wife died more'n twelve years ago now. She just ain't available for no new picture, that's all. You see what I mean?"

"Yes, sir. I sure as hell do!" I lit a cigarette, shoved the pack in Adamski's direction. He shook his head and smiled.

"I never touch 'em myself. I don't smoke and I don't chew

and I don't go with girls who do!" He winked again and smiled. "Ever hear that one?"

"Yeah. Our class won the Bible. But I've never heard of any man celebrating his fiftieth anniversary without his wife."

"Mr. Jessup did," he said sternly. "It was all wrote up in the Sunday paper five or six weeks back."

I closed my eyes and rubbed them, thinking back. No, thank God! I hadn't written the Jessup anniversary story.

"If that got into the paper, Mr. Adamski, it was a mistake, and we'll have to print a retraction. The way it's supposed to be," I explained gently, "both members of the marriage are supposed to be *alive* on their fiftieth anniversary."

"I always thought that, too." The old man's lips trembled; his eyes were very bright and close to tears. "But when old man Jessup got his write-up, and he's been showin' it around down to the cardshed to every fool that'll look at it, I didn't see no harm in me getting a little notice too. I'm as good as he is, and I'll beat him two out of three games of checkers every day but Sunday!"

"I'm sorry, Mr. Adamski." I closed the scrapbook, and placed it in his lap.

"Can't you make no exceptions?" he pleaded.

"Not very well. I'm sorry as hell, Pop. It's a crazy rule, I know, but the paper has to draw the line somewhere. You can see that, can't you?"

"It just seems like yesterday me and Hazel was married." Hugging the huge scrapbook he got wearily to his feet. "And it ain't right! An old fool like Hank Jessup, and..." With a gnarled, twisted forefinger, he wiped his eyes.

"I'll tell you what, Mr. Adamski. This week I'm pretty busy, but some time next week I'll call on you, and maybe we can work out some kind of feature story—"

"No, thanks." He drew his shoulders back and lifted his chin. "I ain't worth no story all by myself." Holding his back stiffly, he marched briskly toward the stairway.

I went into the M.E.'s office and told him about the old man and the Jessup incident.

"I remember the Jessups," J.C. said when I had finished. "There wasn't any mistake, Hudson. I checked that out myself. Mrs. Jessup looked as if she was dead, but she was definitely alive. Adamski was trying to snow you under, and you're lucky you caught him at it."

"Right now, I'd like to write a story on Adamski's golden anniversary anyway."

"Why?"

"I feel sorry for him, that's why."

"Even with my mushy prostate and hemorrhoids, I am also capable of feeling sorry for an old widower like Adamski. And in your weary style, Hudson, you could write a fairly decent human interest story about the old man. But the population percentage of Lake Springs, counting the retirement village, runs close to thirty percent in residents over sixty-five. These old people take these things seriously. If we ran a faked-up piece on Adamski we'd have to set up a separate Sunday section on anniversary dates for widows, widowers and all."

I grinned. "That isn't such a bad idea, Mr. Curtis. We could also expand the Sunday Women's Section. About all it has now is wedding announcements, engagements, and bride photos. We could very easily add a new section on divorce, with photos of divorcees and their ex-husbands. 'Mr. and Mrs. Smith announce the impending divorce of their eldest daughter, Mary. The beautiful divorced matron wore a dark gray dress, ballerina length, and carried a bouquet of green money. The principal witness, Divorcee Helen Jones Brown Goldstein Henessey, one of Lake Springs' most popular co-respondents—'"

"Haven't you got any work to do?" J.C. said ominously. "If you haven't—"

"I'm going out to the Beachcomber's Club. There's a child psychologist giving a lecture to the Women's Auxiliary, and I plan to pry into Marion Huneker's past while I'm out there. She was a member, you know."

"You should get something. How's Beryl, by the way?"

"Fine. I see my wife every day, and she always asks about you, Mr. Curtis. In fact, as long as I'm on the night shift, she worries because she can't have you out to dinner. She wonders if you'd like to drop by for breakfast some morning?"

"Give Beryl my regrets, but ask her if she'd like to have breakfast with me some morning at the Sealbach Hotel. We have room service there."

"She'll be thrilled, Mr. Curtis. I'll tell her about your invitation the next time I see her."

I left the M.E.'s office, shoved a wad of yellow copy paper into my jacket pocket, and drove to the Beachcomber's Club.

Chapter Four

The Beachcomber's Club was a long powder-blue building on the nicer side of the lake, with yellow ground lights placed haphazardly throughout the tropical grounds, trained into the rattling tops of coconut and royal palms. An enormous patio, flagged with irregular stones composed of mixed coral and concrete, separated the "L" shaped swimming pool and "L" shaped blue-and-white cabanas from the main clubhouse. There was an outside bar for outside parties; and an inside bar–lounge that was closed for cleaning only, between four and six A.M. Two narrow but sturdy piers jutted out at right angles from a wide veranda facing the lake, and members could berth their boats at these piers all year 'round for a reasonable fee.

The annual club membership fee was not reasonable. A single membership was $150 a year, and a family membership was $250. Needless to say, I was not a member.

The original idea behind the establishment of the Beachcomber's Club had been fairly sound, but the original plans fell through, as too ambitious plans often do. While the building was still under construction, six years before, an energetic club committee plugged confidently away at a preconceived plan for permission to have a canal dug from Lake Springs to the Inland Waterway. The funds were available, and if permission had been granted, the members would have been able to leave the lake, sail down to the waterway, and from there to almost any port on the East Coast.

The city commissioners, who were delighted with the idea of having an elaborate clubhouse on the lake, stalled the club members on the canal business, and then turned them down flat when the construction of the swimming pool and club buildings was well under way.

Their reasoning was valid so far as Lake Springs' permanent residents were concerned, although there was still bitterness among the members of the Beachcomber's Club. Lake Springs had a white, sandy bottom; the water was clear enough to spot a lost wristwatch at three fathoms. There were ten to fifteen thousand tourists who came to Lake Springs every year to fish and swim in our delightful lake, and if the water had been turned into a muddy, cruddy blue, which it may have done if a deep-channeled canal had connected it to the waterway, these tourists would have bypassed the lake—or so the hotel and motel association convinced the city commission. The other objection, which had been more practical, concerned itinerant boat bums. If Lake Springs residents could reach the Inland Waterway, the out-of-state boat bums could also reach Lake Springs. And this was a type of pest our city didn't want to encourage. We didn't want our lovely city turned into another Fort Lauderdale, St. Augustine or Stuart....

The pro and con arguments made good newspaper copy occasionally, and I was no stranger when it came to visiting the club. But the twenty-foot limit for boats allowed on the lake had turned the club into a dilettantish social organization instead of the exclusive yacht club it had wanted to become originally.

Not more than one club member in ten owned a boat of any kind. The male members got drunk, played poker, and on Sunday afternoons were coaxed into rhumba and cha-cha lessons in the auditorium. The wives, with more idle time on their hands than their husbands, played bridge, gave tea and cocktail parties, had their minds improved by visiting lecturers, and also got drunk in the bar.

I parked in the front lot, but to avoid the crush of milling women and the reception committee clustered at the main entrance, I entered the clubhouse through a sliding, glass patio door. It was still early, and there were only a half-dozen women in the bar. They must have expected a big night, however, because I noticed that Mel Haight, the Chief Bartender, had hired an extra bartender and two extra lounge waiters. I sat at the lower end of the bar, half-hidden by an unneeded white concrete column, and waited for Mel to break free for a few minutes.

Mel was one of my contemporaries. I was a year older, but we had attended Lake Springs High School together, and we had both served time on the football and basketball teams. Neither one of us had been able to make the baseball nine. Except for this all-but-forgotten sports activity, all we had in common was a nostalgic remembrance of the way things used to be. Not much, but lasting friendships have been formed on lesser ties. I had preserved my hair, but Mel's straw-colored hair had been gone for several years. Mel had gone to work immediately after leaving high school, instead of going to college, so naturally he had forged ahead of me in annual take-home pay. As the head bartender, his salary and tips more than tripled my yearly income. He drove a new Buick convertible, and I drove a five-year-old tudor Chevy.

Within a few minutes Mel came down to my end, reached across the bar, and we shook hands. "You covering this thing tonight, Richard?"

"After I get a drink I am."

Mel dropped two ice cubes into a six-ounce glass, filled it

with Coca-Cola, and smiled as he set it before me. I pushed it to one side.

"I said a drink."

"Wait a couple of minutes, Richard," he said softly. "The manager's over by the arch. They're starting to crack down lately, enforcing a new ordinance. That last rezoning law put the club into the residential section, and the only way we can keep our liquor license is to serve members only. Not even guests can get a drink, unless they're from out of town."

"I'm not in either category. I'm a member of the press, and besides, that ordinance is only a technicality."

"I know, but the Chief of Police is trying to enforce it. He came out the other day and threw a scare into the manager. They picked up a stranger on a drunk-driving charge, and he claimed he picked up his load here. He didn't, but the sweat is on for awhile, anyway."

"Little old Lake Springs is becoming quite a metropolis, isn't it?"

"Nothing's the same anymore, Richard." He sighed. "I had to shell out a thousand bucks in advance to send my boy to military school for six months. And I ain't counting the uniforms I still have to pay for on top of that."

"That's tough, Mel," I said sympathetically.

"And tips ain't near what they used to be either." He scowled, raised his chin contemptuously, in the direction of the women at the far end of the bar. "And now, if they won't let guests drink in here, it'll be tougher yet."

"Times are hard."

"You said it." Mel took my untouched Coke, held it below the level of the bar, and after dumping half the contents into a sink, filled it to the top with bourbon.

I winked, and lifted the glass. "To better days."

"How's Beryl?" he said sincerely. "We never see you people anymore. Margaret was asking about you and Beryl the other day."

"Beryl's all right. But you and I are both working every night; you know how it is."

"Yeah, and now the Season's coming up at the end of the month."

"Maybe we can have lunch some afternoon."

"How about some golf, Sunday maybe?"

"I don't play."

"I can't say that anymore, Richard. The new pro at the club has done miracles with my game. You really ought to take some lessons."

"Maybe so, Mel," I said seriously. "I think Beryl would appreciate that. She doesn't think I get enough exercise."

"You give me a ring, and I'll introduce you to the pro, get you started right before you develop any bad habits. A lot of pros can play all right, but they can't teach. This new guy can explain things. The other morning we—"

"Mel. Did you know Marion Huneker, the woman who killed herself?"

"Pink Lady."

"What's that?"

"Pink Lady. She always drank Pink Ladies."

I laughed. "How do you make it?" I took some copy paper out of my pocket.

"Well, not everybody makes 'em like I do, but I never get any complaints. I use a half-ounce of lemon juice—not lime—and one teaspoon of sugar. Then add a half-ounce of sweet cream and a dash of grenadine. One and a half shots of gin and shake with cracked ice. This strains out to a four-ounce cocktail glass, and I always decorate with a cherry on a stem. A lot of bartenders now, they use a hollow-stemmed cocktail glass, and fill it with grenadine, but that's pretty God-awful. Tell you what, Richard; you wait till after the lecture starts and I'll make you one."

I shuddered at the suggestion. "You couldn't pay me to drink one, Mel, but thanks for the recipe."

"What did you want it for then?"

"I'm doing a follow-up piece on Mrs. Huneker's suicide. And you've given me a good lead. 'Mel Haight, Chief Bartender at the Beachcomber's Club, said that Marion Huneker's favorite drink was a Pink Lady—'"

"Jesus, Richard! You wouldn't put that in the paper would you?"

"Why not?"

"They might blame me, that's why. And it would reflect bad on the club. People might say I got her all tanked up on Pink Ladies and she went home and killed her children!"

"Do you think that, Mel? That Mrs. Huneker got drunk and shot her children?"

"Why else would she do it, if she wasn't drunk? But she didn't get drunk here, I never seen her get loaded even. Most she ever drank, anytime she ever came in here, was two Pink Ladies. But leave my name out of the story, Richard."

"All right. It was just an idea. What was she like, anyway?"

"What're any of 'em like?" Mel said hotly, jerking his thumb toward a group of chattering women. "Mrs. Huneker was just like them, far as I'm concerned. A drink. A drink for me to remember. They don't like it when you don't remember what their favorite drink is, so I remember. It's my job."

"Did she ever happen to talk to you? I mean, sometimes people spill things to a bartender they'd never tell anybody else."

"No, she was a fairly pleasant woman. She must've told me a dozen times or more that she liked the way I made Pink Ladies, and last Christmas she gave me five dollars, which will be five dollars I won't get this Christmas. Once she asked me if I was married and I told her yes. Then she asked me how my wife killed the evenings when I was working, and I told her that my wife stayed home and looked after the children." Thoughtfully frowning, Mel rubbed a fat, pink hand across his lower jaw. "I never thought about it at the time, but I guess I shouldn't have told her that, should I?"

"Why not?" I shrugged.

"You know, she might've thought I was criticizing her for not staying home with her own kids instead of hanging around the club."

"Don't worry, Mel. She'll never report you now."

"That's right." Mel smiled cheerfully, and then frowned. "A guy really has to watch what he says around here. And when they get loaded, it's all I can do sometimes to keep from telling somebody off. Well, I'd better get back to work, Richard."

"Sure. But one more question. Did Mrs. Huneker have any close friends, girlfriends, for instance, among the members?"

"Mrs. Chatham. Gladys Chatham. She's married to the New York lawyer, Mr. Victor Chatham, the guy who came down here about five years ago or so. He's that lawyer who got a twenty-five thousand dollar judgment against the city the time the motorcycle cop ran over that crippled kid."

"Sure, I remember who he is, but I don't know him."

Mel looked past my shoulder across the room, raised his chin. "That's Mrs. Chatham, the blonde talking to Mrs. Barnes."

Turning on the stool, I spotted her easily. Mrs. Chatham was wearing a red-silk cocktail gown that looked as if it had been sewn onto her body. Her face and shoulders were evenly tanned, and her long tawny hair was like a mane down her back.

"She's a real beauty, Mel."

"Now she is, but not for long. She's a lush, Richard. In about one minute she'll be over at the bar asking for a double-martini."

"That's no indication that she's a lush. Maybe she just likes gin."

"There's worse lushes around here, I got to give her that," Mel confided darkly, and went back to work.

The lounge was crowded now; the air-conditioned air smelled like an evenly mixed combination of gin and perfume. For south Florida, the women were dressed rather formally, either in evening or dressy cocktail gowns, and several were wearing gloves. In Birmingham or Atlanta, they would have all worn hats, but they were hatless here, their hairdos fixed in place with home spraying outfits. (I'd killed a fly on the window once with a can of hair spray, and didn't realize it until the fly turned a lacquered black, with overtones of gold...)

I left the bar and searched for Mrs. Scott, the publicity chairman, wondering if she still held that office. For some reason, the women's auxiliary held new elections at least every three months, and it was almost impossible to keep up with current officeholders. I found Mrs. Scott and four more women in the television room, where they had trapped Dr. Seeney. His face was red. There was a drink in his hand, and he seemed to be enjoying the attention he was getting. I took Mrs. Scott's arm, tugged her away from the group.

"Honestly, Mr. Hudson," she apologized guiltily, "I really intended to call you earlier, but I simply forgot."

"I had the lecture date circled on my calendar. Forget it."

"And I've got another confession..." She took a typewritten

list of names from her beaded handbag and gave it to me. "I just don't know who-all is here and who won't show up. So what I did was type a list of all the members in the club. I didn't know what else to do!" Her earnest, brown eyes popped with well-feigned helplessness.

"That's fine, Mrs. Scott." I put the list away inside my jacket. "This will be *our* little secret. I'll put them *all* down as being present for the lecture. That is, unless you think some of the ladies would object to having their names in the story?"

"Oh, goodness, no!" She laughed, evidently pleased with her subterfuge that had worked. She may not have known it, but every publicity chairman did the same thing on women's activities of any size.

"Do you think, Mrs. Scott, I could talk to Dr. Seeney for a couple of minutes alone?" Mrs. Scott put a forefinger in her mouth, looked about nervously. "We could go into the men's room," I suggested, as she hesitated.

"Oh, no, you don't have to do that! I'll get rid of the girls and stand guard duty outside the door for you."

"Beyond a doubt, Mrs. Scott, you're the best publicity chairman the club has ever had." Flushing with pleasure, Mrs. Scott introduced me to Dr. Raymond Seeney, and then shooed the women out of the door, closing it behind her.

"I'm always happy to talk to members of the fourth estate," Dr. Seeney said pompously, now that we were alone. "But we don't have much time now," he added, looking at his wristwatch. "I'm due to speak in ten minutes. I'm sorry you didn't come over to my hotel this afternoon—"

"Don't worry, Doctor. These affairs always start late. It'll take Mrs. Barnes another twenty minutes or so to peel them off the bar. I just wanted to check a couple of things with you. I already have the all-important local angle; a list of names. Now, you spoke in Orlando day before yesterday, and I'd like to know if you're using the same subject tonight?"

"Yes, I am," he said firmly, teetering back on his heels. "And it's a valid topic for today's modern mother. 'Psychology and the Family' is the title of my—"

"Well, thanks Doctor Seeney. I guess that's about all I need."

"I'm afraid I don't understand. Don't you want to know any of my qualifications, something about my background in the field?"

"All that stuff was covered by the Courtney Lecture Bureau handout, Doctor."

"I see. What about pictures?"

"They sent us a mat for a one-column cut. You must be new on the circuit, Dr. Seeney. You are only getting one hundred and fifty bucks for your lecture, and at that price, they send a one-column cut. If you were a five-hundred dollar expert, they'd have sent us a two-column cut. A bigwig, like Bennett Cerf, for instance, gets a truly big play; and we send a staff photographer to take his picture getting out of the plane. But he's a fifteen-hundred dollar man."

The lecturer laughed. "We're all classified, eh?"

"Yes, sir. Sorry if I hurt your feelings."

"No, no, not at all. You surprised me, however. I'm certain you'll enjoy my little talk, though, Mr. Hudson."

"I wish I had the time to stick around and listen to it, too." I stuck out my hand. "But I've got other things to do, I'm afraid."

He pouted slightly and reluctantly shook my hand. "How are you going to report my lecture if you don't hear it? Answer me that!"

"I don't mind telling you, but you're a trifle sensitive, Doctor."

"I am like hell sensitive!" he growled.

"Makes no difference to me." I shrugged. "Here in Florida,

like any other state, the *News–Press* exchanges papers with the other state papers through the mail. A reporter in Orlando covered your lecture day before yesterday, and I got the Orlando paper today. So all I have to do is change the date and place of lecture, and the story's written for me. At the bottom—" I patted my breast pocket "—I add the names of the women here tonight, and that's thirty, Doc."

"That's a damned slipshod way of writing a news story!" he said forcefully.

I smiled pleasantly. "I don't tell you how to lecture; what gives you the right to tell me how to write news?"

"For one thing, your opinion of my talk may be different from the Orlando reporter's. To simply parrot what he says—"

I laughed and cut him off. "It so happens that the reporter in Orlando doesn't have an opinion either. He rewrites his story from the Tallahassee newspaper where you talked to the F.S.U. students. And nobody really gives a damn about what you say here tonight, anyway, if you want the truth of the matter. That cackle of women out there will check the paper to see if their name is listed, and to see if it's spelled correctly; but very few people in town will read the story with any interest. As a Doctor of Philosophy, you should take such things philosophically."

Dr. Seeney exploded with a burst of phlegmy laughter. "You're getting through to me at last, Mr. Hudson! How would you like to join me in a drink? Or do you have to wait for a decision to filter down through Orlando?"

"Some other time, but thanks." We shook hands again. "And I hope they send us at least a two-column cut before you come down this way again."

"So do I, by God!"

The lounge was emptying quickly, although some of the

women carried their drinks with them into the auditorium. Mrs. Barnes, the club president, bustled about officiously, her neat brown moustache limp with sweat, as she coaxed the women out of the lounge. The two waiters were wandering around the room collecting glasses and emptying ashtrays into a pink garbage can. I sat down at the bar and ordered a double-bourbon.

"I missed Mrs. Chatham," I said to Mel, "and I wanted to talk to her before the lecture started."

"She'll be back in a minute." Mel winked. "I told her you wanted to talk to her, and she thanked me for the excuse."

"What do you mean? Excuse."

"Stick around. You'll see." Mel began to pare some lemons for the after-lecture bar rush.

Within two minutes the auditorium door opened; and Mrs. Chatham tripped smilingly into the lounge and came directly to the bar. "Did I forget and leave my purse on the bar, Mel?" Mrs. Chatham had a lovely voice, with an alto huskiness that suggested an ability to sing those thousands of songs all about losing a man for one reason or another.

"No, Ma'am." Mel shook his head. "You left it with me to hold for you." He brought the purse from its hiding place, and placed it on the bar beside my elbow. "This is Mr. Hudson, Mrs. Chatham, the reporter from the *News-Press*." I took the two fingers of the gloved hand she extended, shook them, and then indicated the stool beside mine.

"How do you do, Mrs. Chatham. Could I buy you a—" I put a finger to my nose, and looked at the ceiling as if in deep thought "—a double-martini, perhaps?"

"How nice." She hoisted herself onto the stool, and for a happy moment I thought her dress would split.

"I know you're anxious to learn about psychology and the family, Mrs. Chatham, but if you can spare me a minute or two,

I'd like to talk to you about Mrs. Huneker. You were fairly close friends, weren't you?"

"To a certain extent, yes." She smiled good-humoredly. "But two women, as you should know, can never really be close friends."

She half-turned, and I dodged back instinctively from her full bust. Her potent femininity made me a trifle nervous, and she gave off an exotic scent, a peculiar mixture of gin, tweed and night-blooming flowers. "This isn't really the time and place to discuss the late Mrs. Huneker," I said gravely. "And if it would be convenient, I'd prefer to talk to you privately at length. Tomorrow, or maybe the next day."

"Why?"

"For one thing, her suicide has generated considerable local interest."

"For whom?"

"My editor, for one. While people still remember her, I'm trying to learn why she did it. The readers might be interested."

"She left a note." Mrs. Chatham accepted her drink, "Thanks, Mel."

"The note didn't say very much, Mrs. Chatham," I persisted. "A lot of people aren't too happy about television, but they aren't killing their children and themselves because of the programming."

"You're a very serious young man."

"I'm nearly thirty."

"A serious young man." She hurriedly drained her cocktail, and I marvelled that she could drink that much gin so swiftly.

"Would you like another, Mrs. Chatham?"

"Yes, but I'd better go inside. I'm with a couple of other girls this evening. It was nice meeting you, Mr. Hudson." She extended the two gloved fingers.

"What about—"

"Drop by my house in the morning, but not before eleven. I don't get up any earlier."

"Neither do I."

Mrs. Chatham may have been self-conscious about Mel and me watching her as she crossed toward the auditorium, because she hardly swung her hips. She only partially opened the door to slip through, and in profile, her breasts were unbelievably large.

"I wonder, Mel, if she—"

"In a lousy job like mine," Mel said sourly, "it doesn't pay to make any educated or uneducated guesses."

Without embarrassing Mel by offering to pay for my drinks (I couldn't pay for them without leaving a tip, and to tip an old friend would be an insult), I drove back to the office. I dug through the out-of-town newspapers to find the account of Dr. Seeney's lecture. But I had had a change of heart, and I didn't use the Orlando story after all. Too often lately, I had been taking the easy way, when it wasn't really any more difficult to write the news story in my own blundering style.

For three typed pages I gave Dr. Seeney a big build-up, making the trite things he was probably saying about Psychology and the Family sound as if they were new and exciting, and then I pasted the typewritten list of club members to the last sheet and turned the copy over to Harris. Dr. Seeney had seemed a decent sort, and it was no skin off my nose to give him an overblown build-up.

I picked up my ringing phone, and took some notes from the secretary of the P.T.A. I wrote three paragraphs about the P.T.A. confab and put it in the slot.

A new publicity man from the Toastmaster's Club paid me a

visit, and I took time out to brief him on the type of stuff we wanted.

I looked over a few pamphlets about the TM's that he left with me, found them interesting, and typed up three paragraphs about the aims of Toastmasters.

The deadline was only fifteen minutes away, and there wasn't anything that absolutely *had* to go in, so I called it a night. Carrying my jacket over my arm, I went down the rickety back stairs to the parking lot. For at least five minutes, vaguely depressed, I sat in my car smoking a cigarette.

I left the lot and drove to the long parking area facing the lake, which was known locally as Smooch Park. I was an intruder at this place, parked all by myself among a dozen or so cars containing panting young lovers, but I wouldn't be bothered here. A patrol car made the area every half-hour or so, but the Chief of Police had given his night patrols standing instructions to leave the couples alone—that is, unless they dismounted with a blanket and headed into the neighboring piney woods. Once I had asked the Chief about this hands-off policy, which wasn't very popular among the fathers and mothers of teenaged daughters. "Iff'n young folks don't have no place for experiments," he told me, "they don't never get married." I considered the Chief's doubly-negative approach to young love as rather refreshing, and in some ways, practical. In my high school days, I had done some experimenting at Smooch Park myself.

And thinking back, I still remembered the humiliation of my first experiment, if I could call it an "experiment," in first-hand biological knowledge. In retrospect, checking over the combination of all the various aspects of my initiation, it had been a nightmare all of the way around that could have turned me against sex forever. It had been a gang affair, which meant that

I was surrounded by laughing watchers, all of them older than myself. And worse, being the youngest of the six boys I had been the last in line—except that I wasn't in the line, nor did I get to watch the other five, peering in through the car windows as they took turns with the willing, nay, eager victim on the back seat. No, not me; I had been stationed up on the road as a guard, a lookout, to holler down to the gang at the car in the event of danger. And all of the time I stood by the road, conscientiously looking up and down, with the concentration of a thirteen-year-old boy assigned to hazardous duty, I was filled with anxiety, afraid that the bigger boys would give me my turn when it came. And I was also afraid I would not get a turn.

My anxiety was valid enough. The girl in the back seat of the big black Buick, Gertrude Erdman, had learned through experience that she could receive a certain amount of cash for the very same act that made her so incredibly popular at Lake Springs High when she was putting it out free. Her charge was nominal, only twenty-five cents, but no matter how often I counted my change, as I stood guard duty on the road, my eighteen cents was still only eighteen cents.

But I got my turn; I needn't have worried. The others wouldn't have missed their chance to watch my awkwardness, or to issue jeering advice, under any circumstances.

The dim interior light glowed inside the car, as they pushed me into the back seat and slammed the door, encouraging me to perform feats in the art of love that would have taxed the powers of an immortal Greek God—and there sprawled Gertrude, in all of her unlovely adolescent pulchritude. She had taken off all of her clothes, of course, and even under the dim, ceiling light, it was possible to count every one of the ribs in her skinny, underdeveloped body. Her breasts were as hard, and every bit as large, as twin halves of a green orange. Her face was perspiring freely, and she had pushed back the dark bangs that ordinarily concealed the peppering of pimples and blackheads on her forehead. She knew that I was the cherry—she had picked literally dozens in Lake Springs High during the two semesters she had operated, both non-professionally and professionally—so she smiled at me first, exposing the golden braces on her front teeth, before holding out her hand.

"Money first," she said coyly, "or Gertrude doesn't play." I opened my damp fist, and dropped the moist coins into her hand. And sure enough, she counted it, squinting in the semi-darkness, as I held my breath. But to my astonishment, she said nothing; she merely dropped the change into her purse, which was on the floorboards. A good many years had to pass before I learned that there were a lot of girls in this lousy world who used an open box as a means to obtain affection. But at the time I was merely grateful to her for not announcing my shortage to the others. It was bad enough as it was.

"Go ahead and kiss her, Richard!" McNally advised. "You paid her."

Grinning weakly, I shook my head; the idea of kissing her appalled me. In my mind I could visualize a million germs and food particles on and behind the braces of her teeth.

"Come on, Richard," Gertrude said, spreading her skinny legs and leaning back, "let's get it over with."

The watchers had merely been giggling before; they now laughed uproariously as I attempted, in my innocence, to fondle this frail fourteen-year-old. I was limp with fright.

"Just make believe—Rich," Gertrude whispered, hissing in my ear; because I had no idea of why they were laughing so hard. By the time I got this idea through my head, she had slumped down and grabbed me—and this was my undoing. The car seat received the full fruit of my eighteen-cent charge.

To give Gertrude credit, however, who was certainly aware of the evidence, she played it through, saying nothing, and we pretended for the few moments the others expected the act to take, that everything was up and aboveboard. I was never certain later whether an actual penetration had taken place or not, but the witnesses thought so, and I kept my doubts to myself, naturally. Better to be hung as a goat than a sheep....

I lit a cigarette, wondering what had happened to Gertrude after she left Lake Springs. No one ever really knew where she went; she merely disappeared one day, and after the rumors went the rounds—"She got pregnant and had to leave," "She went to Cuba to work in a house," and other unsubstantiated speculations—her name never came up again in our conversations. Few who had the chance to get to her, and any boy in the school could have made the opportunity available, were completely free from shame—including myself; although I may be reading my own conscience into the others. But she was a girl for the dark places only; no boy in his right mind would be seen with her on the street or in any public place. My first experience with Gertrude was my last, but for weeks afterwards, every time I had a quarter in my pocket, the knowledge that she was available, that I could stop her in the halls at school at any time and make some clandestine arrangements for an assignation, thrilled me with an uneasy mixture of desire and overwhelming shame.

But that was then and now was now. I had parked for the purpose of going over in my mind a few questions to ask Mrs. Gladys Chatham in the morning, not to think about sex—but I now found that to think about Gladys Chatham was to also think about sex. I shook my head in the darkness; the woman was built like a steel latrine, but why think of her—the unattainable, when the attainable was readily available at home?

I started the car, backed onto the lake road, and pointed for home.

The house was dark, but I made plenty of noise as I came in. I undressed in the study, took a long shower, and I was still drying myself when I entered the bedroom.

"Are you asleep, Beryl?" I whispered.

"Sure," she said, "sound asleep."

I turned on the rose-shaded bedside table lamp. She blinked, covering her eyes with her right hand. Beryl was lying on top of the sheets, a beautiful sight with her shorty white, silk night-gown hiked up above her hips. Her long, tanned legs seemed even darker in contrast to the snowy white band across her hips, which began at her navel, and ended just below the smooth joining merge of her thighs. There was another brown band above her navel, and then it stopped where the halter kept the sun from shining against her incredibly white breasts. And the dark midriff band could be seen through her diaphanous nightgown. As I looked down at her, I was grateful for the laws that kept her from getting an overall suntan! The white, white parts were for my eyes alone—

"Do we need the light?" she asked. "Do you plan on reading in bed?"

I laughed. "No, not exactly. I just turned it on to make sure who this strange woman is that I found in my bed. That's all. I had one in here this morning who seemed a little wild."

She giggled. "I'm rather friendly when you get to know me. But if you're going to leave the light on, Mr. Hudson, please drop the Venetian blinds. The neighbors all think that I married you for your money."

I laughed, to please her, although she had made the same joke—if that is what it was—so many times before it wasn't funny. It was too muggy to drop the blinds, which would block the gentle breeze that struggled through the window, so I turned out the light.

We didn't speak, we kissed instead, the inevitable practiced preliminary. Beryl's upper lip was damp, and her silky skin was as warm as a flannel heating pad. It was well after midnight, and yet the humidity made the air as hot as midday. I had cooled off some under the shower, but little rivulets of sweat were flowing again down my face and neck, and my hair was as damp as if I hadn't dried it.

Playfully, Beryl drummed her fingers on my stomach, and then marched downward. "I understand, sir," she whispered sympathetically, "that you have a growth of some kind here?"

"I hope so," I replied, and such proved to be the case.

There were no shortcuts to love-making with Beryl. She was an emancipated female; she knew her rights and demanded satisfaction every time. Ordinarily, I had no particular objections to prolonging the love play, but there seemed to be a ritualistic sameness, a pattern that had developed over the years that had to be followed at all costs; and instead of being fun, it was something of an ordeal to be undergone before I could obtain my own personal gratification. I was almost detached as I went through the motions, anticipating her responses almost to the second as one followed another.

She now began to cover my face with kisses, moving her hips in slow rhythm; this was my wordless cue to comply, and wordlessly I complied. But this time I was unwilling to wait, and I achieved my purpose without giving her any warning. My perspiration had dribbled onto her breasts and belly, and I tried to raise myself, to get away. But I couldn't; she locked her hands behind my head, flinging her lithe body up against me, and glued her open, sticky mouth to mine, making meaningless sounds of pleasure, and begging me not to stop. She was wild, frenzied by the thought that I had finished ahead of her, as tight against me as lichens growing to a rock; and so, in the end, she received the satisfaction she was entitled to—and who was I, a mere husband, to say she didn't deserve it?

Chapter Five

While I was eating breakfast the next morning, my wife made a fresh pot of coffee for a change, and sat down at the table with me. I eyed her suspiciously as she stirred her coffee, but her smile was pleasant and guileless.

"Are you going to review the Civic Theater play tonight?" she asked conversationally.

"Don't I always? I've got two complimentary's, if you want to see it."

"Oh, no," she laughed. "This is one play I don't want to see."

"It's *Lilliom*," I reminded her, "and a near classic. If they do a halfway professional production, you might enjoy it."

"No, not this one." She shook her head. "I read your account of the lecture at the Beachcomber's last night. Was it really that good?"

"Better."

"How's your play coming along, Richard. You haven't talked about it in a long time."

"I may start all over again."

"Not again!" she said in dismay.

"Yes, again. But not this morning. I've got to get going." I pushed back from the table and went into the bathroom for my necktie. As I reentered the living room, carrying my jacket over my arm, Beryl tried to stop me at the front door.

"You aren't taking the car this morning," she said flatly.

"But I am. I've got some interviews to make today."

"I've got a dozen things to do this morning," she protested.

"Then you'll have to ride the bus."

She followed me outside, wearing the familiar, woeful, hurt expression, but she didn't protest any more. I drove away, feeling uneasy inside, as though I had lost an argument of grave importance.

Because of the building materials used in Florida, there is very little difference between a $10,000 house and a $20,000 house. The size of the lot and its location make the difference in price, not the structure itself. Concrete brick and stucco are used extensively in residences because of possible hurricanes, and this gives the homes a certain sameness in appearance, regardless of what the architect tries to do with his materials. The Yankee Snowbird who moves down to Florida to buy a house becomes confused by the wide range in prices between ostensibly identical homes. The differences are so minor they aren't apparent to his untrained eye.

Not even the number of bedrooms can give a clue to the cost of the house. A two-bedroom dwelling often costs a great deal more than a three- or four-bedroom house; and the differences are so subtle that only the builder knows the reasons, and he can't explain them. In connection with bedrooms, I should mention the Florida-room, because it is unique to Florida homes.

This room is an appendage—either built into the original structure or added to the building later—with three screened and jalousied sides from floor to ceiling, and it's the modern counterpart of the old-fashioned, screened sleeping porch. The Florida-room, as a rule, is built onto the back of the house, and from the day it is finished until undeserving offspring inherit the house, three-quarters of the home owner's living time is spent in this one room. His television set, stereo/hi-fi, and vibrator chair are moved to the Florida-room. If it's a large

Florida-room he eats all of his meals there at a glass-and-wrought-iron table, but if the room is too small for a table, he eats his meals on a folding television tray, just like everybody else in the United States.

To show off his wealth in Florida, the rich man can reveal his financial status only through his wall-to-wall carpeting and furnishings, and by adding a swimming pool to his backyard. But in swimming pools, consumer credit has come to the assistance of the man with small means; for just a few extra dollars a month added to his thirty-year mortgage, he can also have a swimming pool in addition to a Florida-room.

Craftsmanship has fallen off to such a poor standard, costly furniture looks little better than the cheaper copies obtained under long-term financing. The wealthy Floridian, who is desperate to show off his money externally, must furnish his home with genuine antiques or early American furniture, mixed with cast-off European relics, and supplemented by ancient Oriental art objects. Knowing these things, I know that the house containing the most beat-up objects belongs to the wealthiest man. The more threadbare the rugs, the more rickety the furniture, the poorer the taste, the richer the owner.

All of this is by way of saying that I estimated that Mrs. Victor Chatham's residence had cost her husband approximately $26,000. If the house had been on the lake, I would have added $5,000 more to my estimate. As I banged the brass knocker on the door—there wasn't a buzzer—I figured the clever architect had pocketed $.85 by this little trick.

"Come in, Mr. Hudson," Mrs. Chatham said smilingly, as she opened the door. "And it's rude to stare, you know."

"I'm sorry. I was thinking."

I followed her through the living room, through glass sliding doors, and into a Florida-room which faced a swimming pool.

The pool was an oval instead of the conventional kidney or narrow oblong, so this meant that either Gladys or Victor was trying to assert some kind of individuality.

"Who built your pool, Mrs. Chatham?"

"We had it put in about a year after the house was finished. The Merlin Marine Company did it in three or four days. It was fun watching them—"

"It took six days," I amended. "And the foreman apologized as he said—'We could finish it by tomorrow afternoon, Mrs. Chatham, but tomorrow's Saturday and I don't want to nick you for overtime. So we'll just leave the mess the way it is, and come back Monday morning.'

"As soon as he told you that you called your husband to get an okay for the overtime so you could have a new pool celebration party Saturday night." I smiled. "Am I right or wrong?"

"Mostly right!" She laughed, a husky, hearty sound, and sat down on a chintz-covered bamboo couch. "Only I didn't call my husband. How did you know this, Mr. Hudson?"

"I know the foreman at Merlin, and that's the way he operates. So your house cost you about twenty-six, five."

"That's close, but it was nearer twenty-eight thousand. I can see you've been checking on me."

"No, not really. Only an estimate by a native Floridian, but I don't know how I missed it that far. I'm slipping, Mrs. Chatham."

"We have a double carport."

"I counted that."

"I know!" She clapped her hands. "My husband's study. It's completely paneled in Philippine mahogany, all matched wood. And you didn't see it as you came through the living room because he keeps the door locked."

"That's a dirty trick to play on an assessor."

"I think so, too," she agreed. "I feel like Pandora sometimes;

I want to go in there so badly. There isn't anything in his old study I haven't seen already, but that locked door is like a challenge to me every day. He's just fussy about his papers, afraid I'd go through his files and mess them up. I wouldn't, but—"

"I think you might," I said solemnly.

She smiled like a mischievous little girl. "I might at that."

"Now," I said, taking copy paper and a pencil out of my jacket.

"Would you like some breakfast, Mr. Hudson?"

"I had breakfast."

"I mean a drink."

"Sure. Either bourbon or scotch with water will be fine."

"You can have both if you can't decide."

"I'll settle for the bourbon then."

While she fixed the drinks at the bamboo bar with the Micarta top ($98.75 plus tax at all Modern Rattan Stores) I put the paper and pencil on the coffee table in front of me. A good interviewer doesn't take notes. I had only brought out the paper as a prop to show that I was calling on business.

"And here we are." She sat down on the couch again, facing me.

"To Marion Huneker," I raised my glass, "wherever she may be."

"I'll drink to that."

Over the rim of my glass I fixed my intelligent eyes appraisingly on the woman. She had evidently made an effort to prepare herself for my arrival, but she hadn't quite made it. Her tawny hair had been brushed, and it swirled about her shoulders with a careless effect. She wore a pair of bullfighter toreador pants that hit her just below the knees, and they were fashioned from a shimmering gold material of some kind. A male-styled white shirt, tied by the tails at her slim waist, was much too large for her, and her formidable bosom wasn't as evident as it had been in the tight evening gown she had worn the night before. The shirt collar was open at the throat, and although she had powdered after a shower or bath, the powder was caked here and there on her neck. These patches of pink caked powder irritated me, as did the woman's oversight in failing to remove a tiny fleck of yellow matter from the corner of her left eye. A "sleepy" is the term for this tiny piece of matter that forms in a person's eye when sleeping. I see too much sometimes, and I was being hypercritical, which wasn't fair...

"Can you give me one good reason why Mrs. Huneker killed herself?"

"You're such a serious young man!"

"Why do you keep saying that?" I said irritably.

"Because you frown so! If you didn't glower, you could be quite handsome, Mr. Hudson."

"Handsome is as handsome does, I always say. It's an axiom we ugly men must live by."

"You're far from being ugly—"

"Well, you're close to being beautiful."

"I wasn't fishing, Mr. Hudson."

"I am. I want to know why Marion Huneker killed herself and her two children."

"Why?"

"My editor has prostate trouble, and he's afraid to go to a doctor because an examination might turn up a cancer. Being afraid of death himself, he is outraged when somebody takes their own life. Especially a well-to-do woman like Mrs. Huneker, who has no apparent reason to die."

"And he wants you to write about her suicide?" Mrs. Chatham wrinkled her nose distastefully. "Isn't that rather morbid?"

"Newspaper readers are a morbid lot, Mrs. Chatham; they enjoy reading about death in every form. We report knifings, matricides, patricides, infanticides, and suicides, and the obituary column is the most popular feature of the paper. On state-sanctioned electric chair murders we send a personal representative, and we describe all highway deaths as colorfully as possible. If we were unable to devote a goodly portion of our pages to wholesome, violent death, our circulation would drop drastically. And without a healthy circulation, we couldn't charge so much for ads."

"I see. But why would anybody be interested in Marion's suicide? Other than morbidly, I mean?"

"Suicide, more than any other form of death, makes people indignant, that's why. The life force is all we have, and when people kill themselves, it frightens the survivors. I think my editor wants me to come up with some valid reasons. If so, we can encourage others to commit suicide, and by reporting their deaths, increase our circulation. Suicide, once it starts, comes in waves, like a fashion. A lot of people, who have considered it but haven't acted for one reason or another, are often encouraged by the brave example of another."

"I'm afraid I don't like your editor, Mr. Hudson."

"He's a good man, Mrs. Chatham. Did you ever see a person murdered, Mrs. Chatham?"

"I've seen dead people before."

"Did you ever witness a death; see someone killed right before your eyes?"

"No, and I don't want to either!"

"Neither did I, but that was one of my first assignments when I started on the paper as a cub reporter. Mr. Curtis is against capital punishment, you see, and to make certain that all of the members of the editorial staff see it his way, he assigns new writers to cover electric chair murders at Raiford. Before I made the trip to Raiford I was merely indifferent to capital punishment, but now I'm definitely opposed to it. After you see a boy of twenty killed in the chair, your realize that it is you personally pulling the switch on him."

"Are you really serious?"

"Yes I am. I'm a voter, and as a voter I should be doing something about getting this penalty abolished. To see such a death is to take it seriously. Every year about one out of five hundred thousand Florida residents die in the chair. I realize that this is a small percentage, but suppose your good friend, Marion Huneker, had failed to kill herself after murdering her children? Would you have been willing to pull the switch on her?"

"I think it's too early in the morning to talk about such hypothetical questions. And really, Mr. Hudson, I don't think I can tell you anything about Marion that could help you."

"Suppose you try, and then let me decide?"

"My husband's a lawyer, as you know, and he wouldn't want my name in the papers in connection with Marion's. I know he wouldn't."

"I won't use your name, I promise. I'm concerned with her motivation, and right now, I'm not even positive I'll use Mrs. Huneker's case for my series. It might be better to make it a Jane Doe story. But either way, your name won't be mentioned."

"If you really think I can help…?"

"How long and how well did you know Mrs. Huneker? As a starter."

"We met the Hunekers right after we moved down here from Manhattan. Mr. Huneker was new here, too, and my husband specializes in corporation law. Jack was one of my husband's first clients; he needed help setting up his business when he was getting started. For awhile, we sort of banded together, both families, but Victor and Jack had nothing in common outside of business. As our circle widened, Victor and Jack seldom saw each other anymore, but Marion and I were still very close, and we got along fine. Actually, Marion and I had little in common either, but she was a friendly person, and I liked her."

"What kind of a background did she have? I know very little about her."

"She was second generation Italian, and very religious, like many Roman Catholic women. Her husband never attended church. Her father owned an expensive men's shop in Philadelphia; not rich, but he was far from being poor. So she had an excellent education, if Catholic schools give good educations. I've never attended a Catholic school—my parents were Christian Scientists, when they happened to think about it."

"What type of mutual interests did you and Mrs. Huneker have then?"

"Nothing specifically. We both talked to each other, and we were interested in what each other said, but I can't think of any burning interest we shared together. This sounds silly, now, as I talk about it. We both subscribed to the Book-of-the-Month Club. I would buy the book of the month and she would buy one of the alternates, and then we traded copies after we read the books. We had them both ways, you see, and we checked with each other to be sure we both didn't order the same bonus books."

"Is that the only reading she did? Book-of-the-Month books?"

"Of course not. We often borrowed books from the library. We have a good public library in Lake Springs, as you know. I was merely trying to think of some specific interest we shared. There must've been others. We swam in the pool at the Beachcomber's, and sometimes we played bridge at the club, or met downtown for lunch and shopping."

"How did Mrs. Huneker treat her children?"

"Like children, I suppose. I don't have any myself, but her

children were well-behaved, and I liked them well enough. Not being around them very often, it was easy to be fond of them. Sometimes she told me things they said that were funny and so on, but she wasn't one of those doting mothers who only lives for her children. That sounds idiotic in view of what has happened doesn't it? I mean—"

"So far you haven't told me a damned thing, Mrs. Chatham."

"You're supposed to be asking the questions," she said sharply. "I told you I couldn't help you, in the beginning." She quickly drained her glass, picked up my empty, and fixed two more drinks. When I sipped from mine I found that this time she had given me scotch and water instead of bourbon. A damned poor memory, in my opinion, but perhaps she was rattled…

"Let's take another tack, then," I smiled and she brightened somewhat. "Doctor Goldman was the Huneker's family physician, I believe, and yet he had no comment to make about her death. Do you know if Mrs. Huneker had a serious illness of any kind?"

"Doctor Goldman's an obstetrician, not a G.P. When little Kathy was still a baby, Marion took her to his well-baby clinic a few times, and I suppose she saw him occasionally for personal check-ups, but she wasn't suffering from any diseases or anything."

"She may have been pregnant. I don't think they're planning an autopsy, but—"

"I *know* she wasn't pregnant!" Mrs. Chatham said firmly. "Her religion settled that matter. Marion wanted more children and her husband didn't. Jack felt that a boy and a girl were more than enough children. So they compromised by not sleeping together anymore."

"That's a foolish compromise."

"That's what I told Marion when she confided all this to me.

But Catholics aren't allowed to protect themselves technically in the clinches...so?" Mrs. Chatham shrugged, and raised her glass in a cynical salute.

"What kind of guy is Jack Huneker?"

"An uncultured slob, but a nice guy. My husband says he's one of the best businessmen in southern Florida. Evidently there's no limit to his capacity for work and drive. He's an ex-construction worker who managed to save a few thousand dollars on jobs around the country. He came down here, borrowed an equal amount from a bank, and built up his business from scratch. He's earning at least thirty thousand a year now, and expanding all the time."

"I don't know why, Mrs. Chatham, but I just can't get a clear picture of Marion Huneker. What did she want out of life, anyway?"

"She already had what most women want, Mr. Hudson. Security. But she was also an idealist in many ways. When she was fourteen, she told me, she wanted to become a nun. And then she studied ballet, and dancing knocked that idea out of her head in a hurry!"

"I fail to see the connection."

"Listen, Mr. Hudson," Mrs. Chatham leaned forward and wet her full lips. "If all of the young girls in the United States studied ballet there wouldn't be any nuns. Ballet makes a woman conscious of her body, and reminds her that it's useful."

"That's an interesting theory."

"Not a theory; plain fact. I studied ballet myself as a girl and I know what I'm talking about."

"So you'd say Marion Huneker was sensual then, and wasn't sleeping with her husband? That's a better motive than a dislike of television. Or did she, by any chance, have a lover?"

"Of course not! And she wasn't sensual either, as you put it.

Marion wasn't particularly happy, but she wasn't unhappy as women go these days. She had too many things to do, I believe, to brood about herself very much. Maybe she sat down finally, took enough time off to think things over, and decided that her life didn't add up to what she wanted it to be. Everybody thinks that way occasionally, but Marion might've carried her conclusions out to the justified extreme."

"You don't really believe that, do you?"

"I'm guessing," she replied absently, "I don't know what to believe. I'm talking about my own life more than Marion's. Without any children to worry about, I have more time on my hands than Marion ever did. I think more than she did, maybe, but I take positive actions to keep from brooding."

"Like for instance?"

Mrs. Chatham shrugged. "Like a drink when I want a drink," she said flippantly. "Like an affair when one is needed." She winked the eye that held the sleepy, stared at me boldly, and drained her glass.

"I can see you aren't overly religious," I laughed, taking her empty glass. I mixed another round of highballs at the bar. When I handed her a fresh drink I sat beside her on the couch. "I'm not getting very far with you, Mrs. Chatham."

"Oh, I wouldn't say that." The expression on her face didn't change, but I detected the challenge in her voice. A thin trickle of sweat ran down my sides from my armpits. I picked up the tiny, inadequate cocktail napkin from the coffee table and brushed it across my damp forehead. In nine years of marriage, I had never been unfaithful, not once, although there had been several close calls. Why? Not from any lack of physical attractions, surely; no man is immune to the unknown, untried charms of beautiful women—or even unlovely women for that matter, when he sees a flash of forbidden thigh, or the invitation in a feminine eye. No, it had always been the fear of becoming involved, coupled with the foreknowledge that if Beryl had ever found out about any outside dalliance on my part she would have been hurt.

But here was an opportunity that was a challenge to my manhood only—no extra effort, no involvements, no pretense that this was "pure love," or any of that type of nonsense; but sex, impure and complicated. My throat was dry, and my voice was unnaturally hoarse.

"Does your husband come home for lunch, Mrs. Chatham?" The question seemed an innocent one, almost casual, but she knew why I had asked it.

"Never," she replied, matter-of-factly.

The invitation, and I recognized it as such, was like a line drawn in the dirt between two boys who really don't want to fight, but have delayed the inevitable by challenging each other to step over the line. It was as if she had said, "We have the time, the place; and the rest is up to you." But it was not a point of no return. She was too calm, too collected, too relaxed, almost indifferent to the matter, one way or the other. And it was this attitude she assumed which brought out the male aggressiveness in me. Indifferent? To me? I'd show her what it meant to act that way with me; before I got through with her she'd be calling, "Uncle!"

I set my glass down. Gladys set her glass down. I turned toward her, examining her impassive face for a hint of any inner excitement she might have, but I couldn't detect anything at all, no clues to her true feelings. I moved closer, and as I put my arm around her she raised herself forward to give my arm the space it needed, and closed her eyes. Our open mouths met, and the hard, muscular thrust of her tongue pried my teeth apart; the kiss continued, on and on, and I seemed to feel some underlying pride in the woman that told me that she would never, under any circumstances, be the first to break a kiss, once it had begun. Fighting for breath, I had to break away.

"Let's go into the bedroom," I suggested huskily.

"All right." She got to her feet, picked up her glass, and grabbed the open bottle of scotch off the bar. I took my glass and the bottle of bourbon, and trailed her down the hallway to the bedroom.

After the prolonged kiss, adrenalin was pumping overtime, and I dried the palms of my hand on my trousers after putting the bourbon down on the bedside table. I sipped my drink and watched her as she stripped off the embroidered bedspread with housewifely efficiency and tightened the bottom yellow nylon sheet. It had happened so quickly, the preliminaries had been so short—no verbal sparring and coaxing whatever—I didn't know what to do first. But as I stood there, feeling like a burglar in a strange bedroom, Gladys finished fluffing up the pillows to her satisfaction, and immediately began to peel down her ridiculous golden toreador pants.

"A mosquito!" she exclaimed with dismay, and she slapped the inside of her creamy white thigh sharply.

I grinned as she scratched furiously away at the reddening welt, but as she looked in my direction I hurriedly affected an expression of concern.

"Before we do anything," she wailed femininely, "you're going to have to find and kill that damned mosquito!"

I took her at her word, but as I searched the room I gradually removed my clothes, including my shoes and socks. A mighty hunter, I finally tracked down the bold mosquito—or perhaps a different one—and squashed it to an ingnominious death on the aluminum window screen.

"Got him." I said.

"Thank you," she said, and without sarcasm.

She lay flat on her back, her hands clasped behind her head, without any false modesty. She had a beautiful body and she knew it. Her heavy breasts were still formidable, but they were not so large, now that she was lying down; they were twin melons, perfectly matched, with blunt pink nipples. Unperturbed by my appraisal she stretched luxuriously, spreading her long legs, and the small dark-red welt on the inside of her thigh was the only discernible blemish on her body, and somehow, it inflamed my desire instead of detracting from it.

But as I moved toward the bed, feeling the cool terrazo floor on my bare feet, I was astonished by the expression in her eyes. Her mouth was smiling, but her eyes were filled with a pure, smouldering hatred—for me, and perhaps for every man she had ever known. Intuitively, I saw behind the hatred to the cause, and there could only have been one cause for such uncontrollable hatred: She knew in advance that once again she was going to be disappointed, that no matter how many times she tried with how many different men, she wasn't going to make it; and that it would be the man's fault, not her own.

I could see everything a little clearer now, the reason for her apparent indifference as to whether I made a pass or not. She was careful, discreet, because she had to be. With a lovely home, a hard-working and money-making husband, the material loss would have been too great a sacrifice to be caught in an indiscretion. And so, realizing full well the power of her beauty and her full-blown sensuality, she could pick and choose, always hoping that the next man would be the one, but prepared for yet another disappointment. I didn't know her husband, but I imagined that he had given up years before. How many had there been, I wondered—a husky, young door-to-door vacuum cleaner salesman, a lusty gas station or garage attendant called out to her house to fix a flat tire, or on a trip, perhaps a college boy hitchhiker for a one-night stand in a motel room. This was a small town, and perhaps her opportunities for affairs were not so many as I had so quickly assumed. Certainly she would have to stay clear of the clutching hands of the husbands of her women friends at the Beachcomber's Club, and the opportunity to get away from town on a trip by herself would be more rare than common.

But what did she expect? Did she expect some door-to-door salesman, whose main interest was in the making of a sale, to turn into the long-awaited skillful lover she so badly needed? Dazzled by his unexpected good fortune, a cat of this stripe would be willing enough, but he would also be certain to disappoint her. And with each new frustration and disappointment, she knew it would be even harder the next time, that the disappointment would be greater than before—but she had to keep trying, and it was getting more difficult to try each new failure.

These were all things that I saw behind those smouldering eyes, and I felt sorry for her, a fatal mistake to make with any woman. But my conquest had been too easy, too simple—there were very few men in Lake Springs as safe as me—and she had probably chosen me as her next partner when I had been introduced to her at the Beachcomber's Club bar.

I sat down on the edge of the bed, leaned over, and touched the tip of my finger to the mosquito bite. "Does that stop it from itching?" I said softly.

"Oh, yes," her fingers gently touched my hair.

"And does this itch, too?" I stroked her leg.

"Yes, yes."

"And here, too?" I kissed a nipple.

"Oh, yes, yes! God, yes!" Her fingers clutched convulsively

in my hair, and I grabbed her wrists, disengaging her hands. I sat up abruptly.

"Let's have another drink and a cigarette," I suggested.

"Damn you!"

She turned her head away from me on the pillow so I couldn't see her eyes, and I laughed. I poured two short drinks, took two cigarettes out of the silver box on the table, and lighted them both. I had no intention of making it easy for her; I was the phallic type, and I knew that a compromise solution would not be the answer, anyway, for either one of us. She was aroused now, and her indifference had disappeared, but she needed a jolting, jarring shock of some kind—and so long as I had been elected, I would run the show for the full term of office.

"Here," I said, passing her the drink and lighted cigarette.

She had recovered her control and she sat up, propping a pillow behind her against the quilted headboard of the bed. I put the ashtray between us.

"Want a little water in that?" I asked.

She shook her head, saying nothing, but concealing her puzzlement at the unexpected turn of events. I watched her eyes, admiring her cool complacency.

"You've never made it, have you?" I said suddenly.

"I don't know what you're talking about—!" she began angrily, her lips twisting contemptuously, but when she noticed that I was serious behind my half-grin, she tossed her head and favored me with a rueful smile.

"Once," she said, "when I was fourteen. But that was accidental, and they don't count, do they?"

"No, and that includes the kind that rides on bicycles."

"But I should!" she said fiercely. "There's nothing wrong with me—!"

"Of course not. Why should you blame yourself for the inadequacy of the male animal?"

"I didn't say that," she said defensively.

"You didn't have to, but after today you'll need a new excuse."

"I've heard that before, too." She tossed off her drink, took a long drag on the cigarette and crushed it out in the ashtray. I started to down mine as quickly, but the moment I smelled the fumes I changed my mind. I could feel the effects from the other drinks already, and if I were to last for the indefinite length of time it was going to take to make good my promise, I needed all the power and control I could muster, because suddenly it was important to me. No longer an independent, extra-marital canter through strange, dark woods; I was a fair knight with a chivalric mission, Sir Lancelot cuckolding King Arthur with Guinevere while he was downtown in the law offices fighting the wars of corporate law.

I put aside my untouched glass, butted my cigarette, and set the ashtray on the table. "What do you know?" I asked, bending over her, weaving back and forth, just close enough to let the nipples of her breasts feel the coarseness of the hair on my chest.

"This," she said angrily, and she had an iron grip on me before I knew what had happened. She pinched my nipples enough to make me flinch. "Like any other man, you wear your manhood on the outside, but you haven't got a damned thing inside!" She let go, rolled to one side, away from me, and then rolled back bringing a doubled fist back with her in a wide haymaker that caught me square in the solar plexus—and hard enough to make me say, "Oof!"

I didn't mind; I was rather pleased by her anger. At least anger was an emotion, which was something much better to work against than a passionless complacence. I caught a double handful of her hair, and twisted her head toward me, but at the same time I crossed my legs to guard the vulnerable area. I kissed her hard, insistently. Her teeth caught my upper lip, but she didn't bite, she merely pinched my lip painfully, and then returned my kiss.

It was a duel now. She was determined not to be the first to break the kiss, and so was I. I forced her back to the pillow, released her hair, and worked a hand down her body; she became now as moist and warm as a southern sea. Our tongues were still entwined, and her lips were now rubbery against mine; her pressure against my mouth was so insistent my lips were all but numb. Our bodies were both damp with the strain, and there was an acrid smell of heated perspiration poisoning the air.

Under the relentless probing, I felt the change in her; she had stopped fighting me, not physically, but it was a mental change that I could sense and even smell, because her very odor changed, turning sweet in my nostrils. The hard pressure of her lips receded, subtly, and the time had come for me to show her there was some manhood inside of me. She made no move to assist me, but it wasn't any problem. Her breath was quickening. Her body now was alive and quivering with joy.

I shut off the present. Her body called me back—but each time I fought it off, making my mind take trips to the seashore, to the zoo, and I even pretended that the pounding was coming from the press run beneath the editorial room, and that I was sitting at my desk reading the funny papers. But—somewhere the crucial point had passed, I knew I could go on forever. She would come up to the precipice, then dodge back again as if she were afraid, but I tightened my arms around her and changed the setting on the metronome to a different rhythm. At last she broke the kiss, noisily, jerking her head abruptly to one side, and the first weak wave broke over the dam. She bit into my neck, whimpered, and the salty waves broke through the concrete of her reserve, one following the other. I tried to follow her then, but I couldn't; I had waited too long.

"I made it," she said, and wiped her wet eyes with her fingers.

I rolled away, and lay flat on my back, trying to catch my breath. I managed a shrug, as she caught up my left hand and kissed the palm and fingertips.

I said mockingly: "I didn't know you were in such a big hurry."

She laughed joyously, and snuggled close to my side, rubbing her face against my chest. "Don't worry, darling," she said softly, "we've got all day if we need it, and I hope to hell we do! "

Chapter Six

At three-thirty that afternoon Mrs. Chatham finally got around to preparing some food for us in the kitchen. Wearing her husband's robe, a yellow, raw silk garment with the initials V.C. embroidered on the left breast pocket, I sat in the kitchen breakfast nook glancing through a copy of Jean Kerr's *Please Don't Eat The Daisies*, while Gladys fried Canadian bacon and scrambled a half-dozen eggs.

"Is this one of the Book-of-the-Month Club books?"

"Yes, I believe it is."

"Is it funny?"

"Yes, I believe it is."

"Is my lunch ready yet?"

"Yes, I believe it is."

We both laughed, not with true amusement, but because we were tired and silly. I fell on the simple fare with gusto. For a few moments we ate silently, and then I tapped the book with a forefinger. "Is this one of the books that you and Mrs. Huneker exchanged?"

"Yes, Marion read it, and we discussed it later."

"I just read a few paragraphs here and there, but it seems to be a very warm and human collection of a homemaker's anecdotes. How could any woman possibly read this book and then take herself seriously as a housewife?"

"A woman can't laugh all the time, Richard. Nobody can. I have always been in favor of first things first, as I've proven to you today already, I believe. But this tragedy has hit me a lot harder than I've let on to you, or even to myself. Marion was a good friend, and I can't help thinking that if I had just happened to telephone her at the time…we often called each other for no particular reason—just to talk, you know. Or if she had called me. If I had called, and if she had told me what she was planning, maybe I could've talked her out of it."

"I don't see how you can blame yourself, for God's sake."

"I don't, not at all. What I mean is this—if suicide is as grave a problem as you say it is, why isn't there an office in every city where a person can call and get comfort? A number that is always available, anonymous, where a despondent person can call and get advice and reassurance from some person gifted in human relations. Don't you think something like that would reduce the suicide rate?"

"It might," I said thoughtfully. "And it's a good point for my series. In Marion's case, however, she could've called her priest and received some comfort. Where were you at the time? Maybe she did call you."

"No. I was right here, arguing with my husband, and he was sitting where you are now. Victor was complaining about the size of our monthly liquor bill, and objecting violently to my plan for breaking even."

"What was your plan?"

"Well, I'm not a very good cook. We eat out a lot, and when we do eat at home I either cook steaks or roasts. So I suggested putting in a freezerful of television dinners I could simply heat and serve—to cut down on our food bills. Frozen TV dinners on weekend sales are only about fifty-nine cents, at most, and the savings each month would be more than enough to cover our liquor bills."

"That's a shrewd, logical suggestion, Gladys, but I'm glad I'm not married to you."

"You aren't any prize yourself." She favored me with a child-like smile. "My husband is faithful to me, at least, and for some reason, you've given me the impression that you wouldn't be—"

"Look," I held up my right hand. "We aren't married, so let's not argue. Let's talk some more about Marion. Is there anything else you haven't told me?"

"No, I can't think of anything, and her motive is still as mysterious to me as it was before. Why do you think she did it, Richard?"

"I'll tell you if I can think of the word." I frowned, trying to remember, groping through cobwebs for a long forgotten word. "Redintegrated!" I said triumphantly. "It's a term I recalled from my college psychology course. Psychiatrists use it for the pleasure principle motives. All it means is 'remembering,' but it has something to do with anticipation instead of achievement. We get little real pleasure from actually obtaining the goals in life we set for ourselves. The real pleasure is anticipatory, and if you don't believe me, ask Dr. Freud."

"But what's that got to do with ready-integration?"

"Redintegration," I corrected her, shrugging. "I'm theorizing, but it's a thought. Suppose that Marion anticipated some kind of an ideal married state with a great deal of pleasure? A successful, well-to-do husband, nice home, two fine children, the whole American Way bit. Could her actual achievement of these things possibly add up to the imaginative anticipation of her youthful dreams? At sixteen, or thereabouts, when Marion first dreamed of all these things, the long-distance goal was a beautiful, and maybe an improbable, dream. So when she finally did get everything she wanted, the goal didn't turn out to be much of anything, you see. But instead of setting new and higher goals of achievement for herself, she probably kept remembering her anticipation instead, comparing it unfavorably with what she ended up with. And of course, the goal couldn't possibly measure up to the original dream. Each day she became more and more dissatisfied with her lot, and then—the grim reality was too much for her, and—"

"You didn't know Marion. She wasn't that deep, Richard."

"How do you know? Perhaps she wasn't that deep consciously, but she might have been subconsciously unhappy. If she could have faced the problem with her conscious mind, there wouldn't have been any problem. It's what we don't know that hurts us."

Gladys laughed. "I always heard it the other way around." She made a wry face, and shook her head. "You've got more faith in this psychology jargon than I have. I just 'redintegrated' something myself. Several years ago, in an attempt to find out more about myself, I took fifty dollars worth of aptitude tests. And do you know what I learned? The psychologist told me that I should be a forest ranger instead of a housewife!"

"Two to one you cheated on the tests."

"You win. I did."

"It figures. And I'd better get to work, I'm cheating on the job." I called the city desk on the wall telephone. I asked Harris to tell the M.E. that I was going to the airport and wouldn't be in the office until around five.

"You really are going to the airport, aren't you?" Gladys said sharply, as I racked the receiver. "You can't hang around here, you know. My husband gets home at six, and I've got several things to do."

"I'm leaving as soon as I take a shower. Don't you ever read the *News-Press*?"

"Only the ads. It's a terrible newspaper."

"You're missing a lot then, if you don't read my wonderful sometime column, *Up In The Air* with Richard Hudson. I say 'sometime,' because it isn't scheduled regularly. About two years ago we were getting so many handouts and releases on airplanes, rockets, jets and so on, I got the idea to use some of this gratis stuff in a column. I broached the subject and the M.E. said to try it. So now, when I have enough handouts I write the column. To localize it I lard the column with wonderful tidbits of information from local C.A.P., V.A.R.T., and E.T.C. units concerned with flying and fliers. And once in a while I drive out to the airport and talk to my spies. Items such as, 'Mr. and Mrs. Benjamin C. Benjamin, 9445 Lee Court, flew to Cincinnati to visit their grandchildren,' and other vital earth-shaking news."

"Sounds like a fascinating column. I don't know how I ever missed it."

"I haven't written one for more than a month, and I've got a mass of material on hand. And sometimes, when I do write one, it isn't used."

"Doesn't that make you angry?"

"Nope. Every day I write a respectable amount of copy. The items that aren't used doesn't mean they're any worse than the stuff that is used. I write local stuff, but any halfway decent national story can crowd it out."

"Just for fun, I think I'll watch for your byline from now on."

"It's mostly junk, Gladys. Tonight, for instance, I'm covering the first play of the season by the Civic Theater Group. This is a field I really know something about. I majored in speech and theater arts, but even here I cheat. No matter how rotten a community theater production happens to be I unfailingly give it an excellent review."

"Most of the Civic Theater plays are good."

"That's true enough. They've had a very good director for the last two seasons. Bob Leanard, a Chapel Hill graduate, and he worked in Nashville for three seasons before he came here. In many ways I envy him because he's doing what he wants to do, even though he works like hell, and only gets twelve hundred bucks for a season of four plays. He gets impossible performances sometimes out of the amateur talent he has to work with. Have you met him?"

"No, I don't think so."

I poured a glass of tomato juice, added salt, a dash of tabasco sauce, and considered…."What're you doing tonight, Gladys?"

"No plans."

"Meet me at the theater at eight-ten. I've got a couple of reserved seats, and you might like to see the show. It's Molnar's *Lilliom.*"

"That's a rather ambitious play for amateurs, isn't it?"

"Not if they can learn their lines. Bob Leanard has one advantage that Broadway directors don't have. He doesn't have to use stars and Equity actors; he has the entire city to cast a play from, and he uses people who physically, at least, fit the parts. Anybody can try out for a Civic play, and he always gets a big turnout on casting night."

"Do you ever do any acting, Richard?"

"Not anymore, although I did some at college. I'm on the night shift for the *Morning News*, so I couldn't act now if I wanted to."

"Something you said a moment ago is beginning to register. Why do you always write a good review? If the production is really bad, isn't it cheating to encourage people to see it? Even though the seats are only a dollar and a half, as I recall, to—"

"I know, I know." I shook my head impatiently. "It just happens that the Civic Theater is the only theater group in town. Four measly plays a season, and each play only runs for four nights, Wednesday through Saturday. At the end of the season they're lucky to break even. And they wouldn't do that well if a few rich people didn't kick in with a few checks in order to be listed on the program as patrons. What's a lousy buck and a half when there's only one fabulous invalid in the entire city?"

I laughed, snuffling through my nose, a loathsome habit I wanted desperately to get rid of—but every now and then the snuffling laugh escaped when I least expected it.

"You want the real reason?" I went on. "Okay. I'm writing a play, and one of these days it'll be finished. And when it is finished I want to have the Civic Theater in my pocket for a production. If I'm a proven, staunch supporter of the Civic Theater, they'll more or less be forced into producing my play when it's ready, you see. And before it'll ever have a chance for Broadway, I'll need to see it staged, even by an amateur group, in order to discover weaknesses and lines that need changes. And, too, I'll have four nights of audiences' reaction as a guide. That's the real reason I'm beating the drum for our local director and his lousy amateur actors."

"You're a devious man as well as a serious one, aren't you?" Gladys laughed.

"True, true, and now to the showers."

I showered, dressed, and used a liberal amount of Mr. Chatham's oily pomade on my unruly hair before rejoining Gladys in her shiny, gadgety kitchen.

"You didn't say if you were coming tonight, Gladys," I reminded.

"I'll be there. About eight-ten?"

"Right. In the lobby. You'll have to bring your own car because I can't take you home. I have to rush to the office to write my review for the deadline. But here's one advantage I have over New York critics. Except for revivals they can't study the plays beforehand in the texts. I have a full month to read the play before it's staged, and it's always an old play in book form. I can study the plot, search out the playwright's essential meaning, and so on. If I wanted to, I could really write a beautiful review. I know *Lilliom*, for instance, backwards and forward, and can you let me borrow five bucks?"

"What's that?" Gladys said sharply, narrowing her eyes.

"I usually get a couple of dollars from my wife in the morning, but today I left in a hurry. I'll need some dough for dinner later."

"Oh. Will you pay it back if I give it to you?"

"Probably not."

"I'll let you have three then, not five." Gladys found her purse and parted with two one-dollar bills, and not quite a dollar's worth of change. "Here, you no-good reporter," she said with genuine amusement, "but I'd rather give *you* three dollars than to have you offer it to me."

"Thanks. And by the way, why in the hell did Mrs. Huneker kill herself?" I said casually.

"If my husband comes home unexpectedly and catches you here, you'll have the chance to ask her personally." Gladys walked me to the front door, a possessive arm encircling my waist, the way women do after they give you a little money. "On your next visit, Richard," she said gaily, "if you make one, park that beat-up Chevy two or three blocks away."

"Yes, sir, Mrs. Chatham." I kissed her goodbye.

"Thanks for the demonstration, Mr. Hudson!" Gladys sang out when I was halfway down the walk to my car. "But I already have a good vacuum cleaner!"

I grinned and waved back.

Gladys wasn't really trying to fool the neighbors, and both of us knew it; and she didn't call out that way for the benefit of the old Negro gardener sitting on the curb across the street, who was feeding himself a snack of cornbread out of a paper sack.

She didn't give a damn, that was all. As I drove to the airport I reviewed our three or four hours together, wishing there were more women like her in this false and fakey world, but I came to the conclusion that most men weren't broad-minded enough to accept women like Gladys. Not yet. We men got what we damned well deserved…

Lake Springs was served by one scheduled and two non-scheduled airlines. In addition to a fairly decent terminal, there were two beat-up hangars for the bankers' half-dozen private planes in the community. After talking to a couple of ticket clerks I climbed the stairs to the manager's office on the second floor. Johnny Garner, the manager, was an old pilot, who had served in World War II as a service pilot with a commission as a captain, and was considered a permanent part of the airport. He was an all-around nice guy, with a round, hard paunch, and a deceptive look of vacancy in his blue eyes.

When I pushed into his office without knocking, carrying two paper cups, each of them half-filled with water from the hallway cooler, Johnny removed his feet from his desk and reached into his file drawer for a pint of blended bourbon. "Thought you'd forgotten all about us out here, Richard," he said fraternally, as he added whiskey to the paper cups. "As my favorite actor, Jack LaRue, said on television late, late last night, 'Long time no see.' And it was a good movie, too. Jack LaRue—now there's a man who really knows how to run a night club. It almost makes you want to see Prohibition come back."

"A 1930 movie?"

"No, 1932, I believe."

"What's new?" I grimaced as I sipped my drink. "I promised last time not to mention that whiskey and water tastes worse in a paper cup than it does in a glass."

"Planes land and planes take off." Johnny shrugged. "There

is one thing though," he added seriously, "and if you give it a decent write-up I'll consider it a personal favor."

"I'll write it, but I can't guarantee it'll be printed."

"It'll be printed," he said strongly, leaning forward and resting his elbows on his desk. "You know Old Lady Pritchard, don't you? Blanche Pritchard?"

"Of course. Who doesn't? I know her husband better, though. He's the ticket-taker at the Sunshine Theater, a nice old guy. He's the only ticket-taker in town who makes an effort to learn the names of all the patrons. You'd think he owned the theater, but he only makes about thirty-five bucks a week."

"And he doesn't need any money. He's got plenty; I happen to know. But here's the story. Mrs. Pritchard was here to see me this morning; she caught the ten-oh-five to Atlanta—"

"I got that downstairs."

"That isn't the story. In many ways the old lady's something of a nut, but all the same, she broke down in here this morning and cried like hell. And damn it all, I feel sorry for her."

"Is her sister seriously ill?"

"No, but she's had a death in her family, and I mean the G.O.C., the Ground Observer's Corps. Now that the Air Force doesn't need the G.O.C. any more, Mrs. Pritchard's lost the sole purpose in her life. She kept the G.O.C. going in this town for the last ten years almost singlehanded. She's logged more than thirty-five hundred hours in the courthouse tower, looking for enemy airplanes, and now they say observers aren't needed any longer. All these years she's been going all over town, ringing doorbells, drumming up volunteers, talking to women's clubs, boy scouts, anybody who'd listen to her. She even trapped me into taking turns in that tower for three weeks. You never knew that I was hooked on that, did you?"

"In the beginning a lot of people were hopped up on the G.O.C."

"That's the point. In the beginning. But the last seven or eight years has been a different matter. In Lake Springs, Mrs. Pritchard *was* the G.O.C.! Without her, they would've been out of observers long ago if she hadn't pushed it. It was her baby and she nursed it to her withered old bosom. And now that it's gone she's lost her whole purpose in life."

"She's got a husband," I reminded him.

"Yeah," Johnny said dryly, with a little laugh. "A nut. An old man who wears a two-hundred-dollar tailor-made uniform to take tickets at a second-rate movie house."

I laughed. "Is that right, Johnny? I knew he wore a fancy uniform, but—"

"It's a fact. Mrs. Pritchard told me herself."

"Well, I suppose the old lady deserves some credit for her work with the G.O.C. If you call me when she gets back from Atlanta I'll do a feature story about her."

"Good. And how about an editorial?"

"I'll tell the M.E. He writes the editorials, when we don't use canned ones."

"Thanks, Richard. Let's have another drink."

On the way back to town I stopped for a hamburger and a cup of coffee at a drive-in. I bit well into my hamburger, almost biting past the small coin of meat, as I happened to think of Mrs. Huneker and the parallel between her death and the loss of Mrs. Pritchard's beloved G.O.C. Maybe Marion Huneker had also lost something or other without warning? Something she was unable to replace with anything else? In my future interrogations, perhaps I should try to develop that line of questioning. There didn't seem to be a damned thing to go on so far. It was like a fresh bulb in a string of Christmas tree lights. When one went out they all went out, and you had to try every socket on the string before you found the dead one...

Instead of blinking the lights for the carhop I honked the horn.

"Why in the hell don't you people put some meat in your hamburgers?" I snarled at the vapid blonde in red pedal pushers, as she removed the tray from the door.

"See our sign?" She pointed indifferently. "We've sold more than fifty million hamburgers and you're the first customer who ever complained."

"You say that like you memorized it."

"Well, what do you expect for a fourteen-cent hamburger?"

"How many hamburgers do *you* eat here in a day?"

She smiled, licking her lips. "I may work here, mister, but I don't eat here."

The gag was old, I know, but I laughed anyway. And I needed a laugh of some kind to face the evening ahead.

Chapter Seven

"That's a very touching tale, Hudson," J.C. Curtis said sourly, after I finished outlining the Mrs. Pritchard story to him in his office. "I'm perfectly willing to give the old lady some belated recognition for her work. And I'm proud of you for smelling out the story—which I should've done myself. But the real tragedy here is the husband, in his two-hundred dollar fancy uniform."

"I don't see the connection."

"Why does he wear it? He's a retired insurance executive on a more than adequate income. He wears it because he needs a sense of importance, and a bright red uniform fills the need. Now. Suppose Blanche Pritchard, his wife, had devoted as much time and effort to her husband during the last ten years as she did to the G.O.C.? By building up her husband's ego instead of some abstract government alphabet ritual, her husband would be a happy man in his own right."

"Hell, he's happy now."

"That isn't the point, Hudson. True happiness, shared happiness, is not the same as manufactured happiness."

"The results are the same, aren't they?" I shrugged.

"Do you really think so? Give me an example, then."

Rubbing my chin, I tried to think of one.

"Then get back to work," J.C. said sharply. "I can't waste my time on you any longer."

"Yes, sir." I turned to go but he stopped me.

"Just a second. Here are some more clippings for you. I went through some old out-of-state papers and cut them out. There are nine different stories here, where men shot and killed their wives, mothers, or children, and then themselves. An interesting pattern, very. In these cases they were all men of action, and none of them left notes. In suicide, when they go alone, without taking members of their family along, a note is left invariably. But not in these murder–suicide cases—"

"What am I supposed to make out of that?"

"I don't know, that's up to you. But Marion Huneker was a murder–suicide case and she left a note. That's out of the norm, but then, she was a woman. You should be able to make a graph of some kind, and we can have the advertising department do some artwork for it. A nice chart of statistics, something to back up your detailed survey—"

"All right, I'll see what I can do," I growled.

"How is your investigation progressing?"

"I interviewed her best girlfriend today, at full length."

"Did you learn anything?"

"She subscribed to the Book-of-the-Month Club."

"Excellent! What else have you uncovered?"

"Mrs. Huneker was rather fond of a drink called the Pink Lady."

"Fine! Might be a good title for the article. No, too obvious. Godspeed, boy!" He waved me away with a flick of his small hand.

I always took considerable pains with my column, *Up In The Air* with Richard Hudson. The Aviation Writers of America had written me a complimentary letter about one of my columns, and it had spurred me to do my best after that, I suppose. I often went so far as to re-read what I had written and to rewrite items that might be challenged on the grounds of clarity, if not fact.

I turned in my completed column to Harris with instructions to either run it the way it was written or not run it at all. He grunted unintelligibly, and I drove to the Civic Theater.

The Lake Springs Civic Theater was not a converted barn; it was a converted garage. The building had been willed to the city by its former greasy owner, and the Civic Theater, which had been putting on plays in the high school auditorium, had asked for and received the use of the building as a theater. The group was rejuvenated after acquiring the new building. Volunteer manhours of work, in addition to many donations from merchants, had transformed the old garage into an attractive little theater. There were three hundred seats, an outside patio with a few scattered potted palms where coffee was served during intermissions, and an almost adequate parking lot.

I parked in a space near the exit, and looked for Bob Leanard, the director, finding him in the shallow lobby giving final instructions to the ticket-seller. Bob was twenty-eight, but he looked much younger. He wore a straggly black brush on his upper lip, and a matching triangular patch of hair beneath his lower lip. His face hair looked as if it were dyed because his crewcut was reddish, streaked with strands of yellow. The fact that his shaggy goatee made his face resemble an unkempt armpit was his problem, not mine.

"Man, I sure could've used you in this play," Bob said, as we shook hands. He took my elbow and squeezed it gently. "Let's go out on the curb for a smoke. This has been one hellova week, but it's the stage manager's baby now!"

After we lit up I grinned and said: "A theatergoer told me today that *Lilliom* was an ambitious venture for amateurs."

"I think you'll be pleasantly surprised, Richard. It was my idea to use it as an opener, so it had better be good. As usual, the board wanted to open with a comedy, but the royalties for anything decent are high as hell, so I convinced them to play *Lilliom* instead. If this goes over, next time we can play *Will Success Spoil Rock Hunter?*"

"I'd rather see a varied program," I said thoughtfully, "instead of all comedies, no matter how much they make."

"Yeah, but it takes money, money, money, Richard. I'm with you; I'd do Sheridan, Saroyan, and Shakespeare if they'd let me, but I know nobody would come to the shows."

"I would, Bob!" I laughed.

"Yeah, you bastard. You get in free."

"And tonight I'm bringing a guest. Mrs. Chatham, and she wants to meet you. You might write her one of those nice form letters encouraging her to become a patron."

"I've got to get backstage in a minute."

"Don't worry. Give the stage manager a free hand."

Bob sighed, fingering the triangle of hair under his lip. "I'd better start turning things loose, anyway. I won't be back next year."

"I didn't know that. The board isn't bouncing you, is it?"

"Oh, no! Television. I finally got the call, and progress is my most important product. In February I'm going to Waco, Texas to direct television. No more begging for little theater jobs, borrowing furniture, explaining the obvious to bigoted boards. All I'll have to do is push buttons in a control room."

"Yeah, and you won't like it, Bob. *This medium, blue-eyed baby without conscience. Fallowed be thy fameless frame.*"

"What's that from?" He raised his dark eyebrows.

"It's a couple of lines from my play," I said self-consciously, feeling my face grow warm. "I don't know if I told you or not, but I'm rewriting it in blank verse."

"Sure, I remember. You said you were thinking about that last year. How's it coming, anyway?"

"Slow, slow."

"Stick with it, Richard, and if you like, let me see it sometime.

I'd like to have you drop by the theater some afternoon anyway, so you can see what the playreading committee did to *Rock Hunter*. They did a blue pencil revision and removed every single reference to sex! It'll run about forty minutes short, and it's a short play anyway. It'll be about as funny as a rubber crutch. And that, my critical friend, is the next Civic Theater production! Me for television."

I laughed, but I wasn't surprised. The nine-member Civic Theater board had five Methodists and four Baptists. I shared his disgust, however, and we were discussing the cuts and possible repairs he could make when Gladys Chatham arrived.

"What's all this?" she said smilingly, taking my arm. "Something that's almost as good as sex?"

"Ho, Mrs. Chatham," I grinned. "This is Bob Leanard."

After the introductions Bob Leanard excused himself and went backstage after all—he wanted to be certain the curtain arose at 8:40. Gladys and I went through the theater and out onto the patio where we could sit down. The talk with Bob had depressed me, and I must have looked glum.

"I'm sorry I'm late," Gladys said. "Didn't you expect me or did you expect me?" she said lightly as we sank down on a bench beside the lily pond.

"I only wanted you to come early so you could meet Bob Leanard," I replied, truthfully. "In a way, I expected your husband to be with you."

"You didn't ask him, you asked me. Did you expect me to sit in his lap?"

I grinned and shook my head. "You can usually get another single, even on opening night."

"Well, when Vic came home, I demanded that he take me to the theater. To demand is to challenge, and he refused automatically; so I came alone."

"Why do married people fight so much?" I sighed.

"I don't know, Richard." Gladys patted my hand lightly. "It's an occupational hazard. I hate it, but once it begins there isn't any way to end it."

"I suppose." I changed the subject and told her about Bob's decision to quit at the end of the season, and gave her some background on his reasons.

"Is that why you're so gloomy?"

"I like Bob." I nodded. "He's a good director. And I know damned well he isn't going to be happy in a Texas TV station. He won't be doing any real directing, not like he's accustomed to in little theater. It'll be a grouping of a few western music guitar players, or something like that, but nothing creative. And I know he won't like it."

Gladys laughed. "And besides, you had already selected him in your mind to direct your own play, hadn't you?"

I grinned. "That thought had crossed my mind."

"I may not know you too well, Mr. Hudson," Gladys said, fluttering her eyelashes with a false coyness, "but I'd be surprised if you didn't have a few sexy scenes in your play. How would you get them by the Civic Theater board?"

"My play's in blank verse. The sex scenes are much too subtly written to be spotted by Baptists and Methodists."

"I like selfish men; they're so practical."

"That's the first time I've ever been accused of being practical."

We went inside, picked up programs, and I led Gladys to my regular seats, which were on the aisle in the row beside the exit to the parking lot. When the curtain came down on the last act I had to get out fast to write my review before the deadline. I shoved my program into my pocket for future reference, and nodded to a few acquaintances in the audience.

"Beryl Hudson," Gladys said, studying her program. "Is she any relation to you?"

"In a way. She's my wife."

"Why didn't you tell me your wife was playing the lead? She's 'Julie,' and that's the female lead, isn't it?"

I snatched the program rudely out of her hands, searching the cast of characters with a trembling forefinger. BERYL HUDSON leaped off the pages in boldface type.

"What's the matter, Richard?" Gladys said anxiously. "Are you ill?"

"No," I said hoarsely, shaking my head. "Surprised. I could lie to you, but I honestly didn't know my wife was in the play."

My bewilderment was sincere, and Gladys giggled with delight. At that moment the houselights went down, and she had to stuff a balled-up handkerchief into her mouth to stifle her glee.

I didn't applaud the set like the others; I was benumbed. Tiny sharp needles pinged into my arms, my legs, and then pricked my chest. My face was blazing with fire, and my body was cold. I shivered for a second, and then got control of myself.

Beryl can't act! my mind screamed silently.

And she couldn't act. She had been in her high school graduation play in Gainesville, but that had been many years ago, and she had only played a walk-on part at that. This wasn't enough background to play the lead in a tough play like *Lilliom*! Bob Leanard was either trying to get revenge on the board of directors, or he had lost his mind. And then I cursed him beneath my breath for not telling me.

I wondered whether the secret had been his idea or Beryl's.

To be on the safe side, I cursed my wife beneath my breath.

What hurt my feelings more than anything else, sitting there in the dark, tense with anticipation, was to watch my wife pull it off—and she did so, beautifully.

Beryl had the typical untrained soft southern voice, with every bad habit of speech there is: hesitations, indistinct phrasings, poor or little projection, maddening slowness, ignored "ing's," and mispronunciation. She always said "chirren" instead of "children." Of course, I could tell that Bob had drilled her in projection, but from time to time she forgot all about it, and her soft voice dropped way down. Then, remembering that she was supposed to speak up, she would raise her voice again, and there would issue forth a tremulous, shivering undertone, caused, no doubt, by a combination of stage fright, fear, and lack of confidence; and the knowledge that I was in the audience, alert for every mistake she made.

In the part of Julie, however, this quavering tremolo was quite effective, and definitely in her favor. Julie, in *Lilliom*, is, beyond a doubt, the most sympathetic part that has ever been written for a woman. Julie marries a worthless, philandering braggart, becomes pregnant, and then her husband is killed when he attempts a poorly planned hold-up. The unrepentant husband then goes to Heaven or some other unlikely place; fantasy sets in, and the Justice of the High Court or Purgatorio, gives him one chance to return to earth and commit at least one decent act before his final judgment. He is returned for one day, and now his daughter is in her young teens. After talking to her helplessly for a few moments, Lilliom ends by slapping his daughter across the face. Back the poor devil goes to Purgatory…

The final scene, when it is performed correctly, will jerk tears out of the eyes of a Finance Company Branch Manager:

LOUISE: What has happened, mother?
JULIE: Nothing, my child.
LOUISE: Mother, dear, why won't you tell me?
JULIE: What is there to tell you, child? Nothing has happened. We were peacefully eating, and a beggar came who talked of bygone days, and then I thought of your father.

LOUISE: My father?

JULIE: Your father—Lilliom.

> (*There is a pause.*)

LOUISE: Mother—tell me—has it ever happened to you
            —has anyone ever hit you—without hurting you
            in the least?

JULIE: Yes, my child. It has happened to me, too.

> (*There is a pause.*)

LOUISE: It is possible for someone to hit you—hard like
            that—real loud and hard—and not hurt you at
            all?

JULIE: It is possible, dear—that someone may beat you
            and beat you and beat you—and not hurt at all.
            (*There is a pause. Offstage an organ grinder
            grinds away, and the curtain ends the play.*)

Beryl had never looked any lovelier in her entire life, not even when we were first married. The long old-fashioned white dress, the parasol, and her long, soft hair falling to her shoulders, made her resemble a portrait by Gainsborough; and the pancake make-up successfully hid the tiny sun wrinkles around her eyes. I didn't need Gladys to remind me of these things when we went out onto the patio for a smoke at the end of Act One.

"Your wife is beautiful, Richard. And you must be very proud of her tonight!"

"Yeah," I replied noncommittally.

"You sort of robbed the cradle, didn't you, sport?"

"Beryl's twenty-seven. If you call that robbing the cradle!"

"Honestly? She doesn't look more than nineteen or twenty."

"I'll get us some coffee."

At the end of Act Two I didn't go outside for any conversation with Gladys. I went to the men's room instead, and stayed there smoking until the buzzer warned for the beginning of the last act. The second act had given Beryl confidence, and she overplayed hell out of her role in the last act, but even so, tears ran down my cheeks as the curtain started down. I didn't wait for it to lift for the first curtain call, and I knew there would be at least five or six. I patted Gladys twice on the knee, muttered "see you," and scooted out the exit to my car.

I knocked off the review hurriedly, grateful for the feverish activity, but scarcely knowing what I was writing. For a change, I beat the deadline by fifteen minutes. Ordinarily, I was overtime five or ten minutes, and had Harris growling at me. I cut out the cast and credits from my program, pasted them on a sheet of paper to precede my review, and turned it in. With the extra time I had I wrote a two-column head, marked it 24-point Gothic, and gave it to Harris.

'LILLIOM' GRABS GOLD RING
IN CIVIC'S MERRY-GO-ROUND

Harris looked at my head, and then shook his green eyeshade as if there was no hope for me in this world or the next. He slashed slanting lines through the letters, making the all caps upper and lower case, and then made a notation to set the type in Coronet instead of Gothic.

"Play any good, Hudson?"

"Lousy."

"It figures," he said with grim satisfaction, nodding his eyeshade. The eyeshade, the damned green eyeshade! That's all he was, and I'd never seen him without it. Without a greenish cast on his face I wouldn't have recognized Harris on the street. Some day I was going to rip off this eyeshade and expose the bastard for what he really was—the Phantom of the Opera!

Before going home I stopped at Howard Johnson's for coffee and a toasted English muffin. There were some bad, bad days ahead of me—this much I knew—and somehow, I would have to get the upper hand again. Beryl had shown me up as a failure, and she had done it deliberately! But why? Why? Why would she rub my failure to finish my play into my face? By some grubby feminine instinct she had chosen the perfect way to show me up as a flunked-out phony playwright. My name—as far as Lake Springs was concerned—was now a cipher, a large round O!

And the lines—all of those lines she had learned, memorizing them in the only way lines can be learned, saying them again and again and again. When had she found time to do all this, and how could I have failed to notice? For the past five weeks there had been at least three night rehearsals every week at the theater, and she had managed to attend them without me tumbling onto her activity. Of course, I worked at night, but even so…yes, this only proved to show how little the people in this town thought of me! No one, not a soul, not a single friend, had passed me the word. And all this time I had considered Bob Leanard one of my best friends, a guy who was always willing to drop whatever he was doing and talk theater with me. A damned backstabber! Although my mood was savage, I was under perfect control when I got home. The front door opened as I drove into the carport, and Mrs. Fredericks laughed thriftily when I got out of the car and cut across the lawn.

"You still look surprised!" she exclaimed happily, moving back from the door so I could come inside the house. "Tell me. Were you really shocked, Mr. Hudson?"

"Oh, yes, ma'am," I laughed hollowly. "Shocked."

"Do you know," she said confidingly, "we had all we could do, trying to keep the rehearsals a secret from you. And once you almost caught us. Last Thursday night, when you got home before Beryl, I thought we were caught."

"You did?"

"Yes, sir, I really thought so. Remember? I told you that Beryl had asked me to sit because she wanted to see a movie. And then she let the cat out of the bag when she got home by telling you she'd been out playing Canasta. Remember?"

"No. Unfortunately."

"Well, I worried. I really did, thinking you'd surely be suspicious hearing two different stories. But you didn't!" She wagged a plump finger at me. "You didn't! I know I'd never be able to keep a secret that long from my husband. I never could lie to him; he used to catch me every time."

"Yes, ma'am. You girls know how to keep a secret all right." I forced a smile, although I wanted to kick the old lady square in the middle of her ample rear end. But Mrs. Fredericks was really a nice old widow who sat with Buddy for free, when we needed a babysitter, and it wasn't her fault. Mrs. Fredericks honestly believed I'd be happy and excited about a delightful surprise. She didn't know Beryl, that was all. I did.

"Now tell me all about the play!"

I opened my mouth but the old lady stopped me. "Never mind; I'm going Friday night. Your wife promised to get me a complimentary ticket, and I'm taking Buddy with me. And if you told me all about it now, you'd spoil the story for me. You have to hurry now, anyway, because Beryl is expecting you at the party." Mrs. Fredericks found her purse, handed me a slip of paper. "This is the address. They're having a cast party, and I 'spect it's started by now. So just go on ahead and have a good time. Buddy's asleep, and you and Beryl stay out just as late as you like." She tried to push me toward the door, but I didn't budge.

"I'm afraid I can't go, Mrs. Fredericks."

Before I could talk the old lady into going home—she only lived a few doors down the street—I had to argue for fully ten minutes. After she left I poured a double-shot of bourbon and tossed it off. It was medicine, and I needed the shot.

For noise and company I turned on the television set. I had another drink, this time a slow one with water. The telephone rang twice while I debated whether to stay up and fight with Beryl when she got home or to go to bed and fight with her in the morning, but I let it ring without answering it. I decided to go to bed; the more sleep I had, the fresher I would be for arguing. But even in bed I couldn't sleep, and the phone rang a couple of more times, too. No one can sleep when a phone rings. And I kept seeing my wife at the party, a tall gin 'n' tonic in her hand, smiling, accepting congratulations with false modesty— and people asking, "Where's Richard tonight, Beryl? Do you honestly mean he really didn't know you were playing the lead?"

I rolled over and over in the double bed, twisting the sheets, hearing the raucous, mocking laugher of all the rotten amateur actors as it echoed inside my head, and stared blackly into the darkness. I was wide-eyed, and my body was feverish as the hot, angry blood raced at double-time speed through my veins. If I only had a backyard swimming pool to cool off in, I thought—

Gladys Chatham has a pool.

A moment later I was tugging on a pair of khaki Bermuda shorts. I slipped into a pair of loafers, and my hand touched the knob of the front door before I happened to think of Buddy. After all, I was a responsible father, and I didn't want to leave him alone. I opened the door to his bedroom, but he was sleeping soundly; his mouth was open, and his tangled yellow curls were tousled on his pillow. That was another thing that irritated me. Why in the hell didn't Beryl get his hair cut once in awhile? Was she trying to make a sissy out of him or something?

I closed the door gently. The way he was sleeping, not even

dynamite would wake him. The telephone rang again, and it was still ringing as I left the house.

I parked about a half-block away from the Chatham residence, and lit a cigarette without getting out of the car. I felt a little crazy, but I was determined to go through with it—if Gladys was still awake, anyway.

Her house was the second from the corner, and the first house was dark. The houses were well separated on the block, and no one was on the street at this time of night. I circled around the first house, cut through the unfenced backyard, and parted the high Florida holly hedge that separated Gladys's yard from her neighbor's. The light from the Florida-room made highlights on the still waters of the oval swimming pool. Gladys, wearing reading glasses, and a loose-fitting, brightly flowered Kanaka muu-muu, was seated in a bamboo armchair beside the sliding screened doors opening onto the patio, reading a book. Her husband wasn't in sight, at least from my vantage point, but it was quite possible that he was also in the Florida-room and out of my sight line. With as little noise as possible, I worked my way through the hedge with difficulty, managing to lose my left loafer in the process. I felt around inside the hedge, once I was in the other yard, but it was as if the shoe had been swallowed by the ground. I should have left both shoes in the car, I thought; and I gave up the search, removing my right loafer. I put the shoe on the diving board, and padded barefooted around the pool to the sliding doors. My heart was banging madly away, but my fear eased down to a controllable— and somehow pleasant—feeling of apprehension as I ascertained that Gladys was all alone in the Florida-room. Perhaps there is a little voyeurism in all of us, but despite my fear, I enjoyed the dangerous thrill of being less than three feet away from Gladys— just looking at her, when she was completely unaware of my presence.

I may have stood there a full minute, or maybe less, trying to get up enough courage to speak to her through the screen. She had a cool head, but she was a woman after all, and the sound of a voice or a scratching of fingernails on the screen might send her into a screaming fit of hysterics. My courage deserted me, and I was on the verge of turning away when she squirmed uncomfortably in her chair, lifted her head from her book, and looked straight into my face—without seeing me. I could tell by the blank expression in her eyes that she couldn't see me, but she must have sensed my presence, my darker shadow on the patio—or she may have heard the sound of my breathing.

"Hi, Gladys," I whispered softly, "can you come out and play tonight?"

The first thing she did was to remove her glasses. She shoved them under one of the small cushions beside her, as if to hide them, and shook her head disapprovingly. She tried to compress her lips in reproof, but she smiled in spite of her efforts to appear exasperated by my unexpected appearance. She was a damned unusual woman, all right, to remain so cool, even if she had recognized my voice. I moved in close to the screen so she would know that it was I, her playmate of the day, beyond any lingering doubt.

She put a warning forefinger to her lips, and looked over her shoulder toward the hallway. I backed away from the sliding screens to the edge of the pool, and sat down on the steps to the diving board. She slid open the screen door and joined me in the semi-darkness. "You damned fool," she said, more amused than angered, "what are you doing here?"

"Cigarette?" I suggested, holding out my package.

"Don't you dare light a match!" she whispered. "Victor might see it. He only went to bed a few minutes ago, and I know he isn't asleep yet."

It was a wise precaution; the bedroom window opened onto

the backyard patio and pool, and although the window was dark, it was a cinch the Venetian blinds were up on such a hot night. I put the pack back in the pocket of my shorts.

"It's such a nice warm night," I said, "I thought a moonlight swim in your pool would be fun."

"There's no moon."

"I thought of that." I reached forward, caught the loose folds of the unattractive garment she was wearing, and pulled her toward me. I kissed her on the mouth, and she shivered, enjoying, no doubt, the same mixture of fear and delight that I felt myself.

"You really are crazy," she said at last, breaking away from me, pushing me away, her hands flat against my bare chest, and trying to suppress a giggle of excitement. "But then, so am I. Wait a second."

I sat down on the diving-board steps again, not because I wanted to sit down—I wanted to run away as fast as I could—but because my legs were trembling. She crossed the patio to the bedroom window.

"Victor!" She said loudly through the window. "Are you asleep?"

"I *was*, or almost asleep," a deep bass voice grumbled.

"All right, all right," she replied. "I'm going for a swim, and I thought you might join me, that's all."

"Do you know what time it is?" the voice asked angrily.

"Why, no, dear," she said sweetly, "what time is it?"

"It's time to go to sleep! I have to work in the morning."

"I'm sorry I asked you," she apologized. "I didn't mean to wake you. But I'm going to swim nude, so if you get up for some reason or other, don't turn on the patio lights."

"You know I don't like for you to swim nude!" the voice objected petulantly. "If the neighbors happened—"

"In that case," she broke in quickly, "don't turn on the patio lights and nobody can possibly see me! Go on back to sleep. I'll try not to splash too loud so you won't be bothered."

Almost simultaneously, the jalousied window slammed closed, and the Venetian blinds rattled shut, as her husband put an end to the conversation. She removed the loose gown as she crossed back to the pool, tossed it down on the flagstones, and dived from the edge of the rounded gutter into the water. I let my shorts fall, stepped out of them, and almost dived myself before I realized that the splash of one dive immediately followed by a second, might be suspected—if her husband could hear the separate splashes through the closed window. I lowered myself silently into the water instead.

Like most native Floridians, I am a good swimmer, but so was Gladys. It was a dark night, and although there were occasional splashes of light on the pool's surface from the well-lighted Florida-room, Gladys managed to elude me time and again in the dark water by surface diving and swimming underwater in unexpected directions.

It was a good game, made even more exciting by the cautious silence with which we played it. The ever-present danger that her husband might possibly decide to investigate the sounds of splashing, or turn on the overhead pool lights from inside the house—despite her warning not to do so—added spice to the game of underwater hide-and-seek for both of us.

But I caught her at last, in the deep water. Gladys giggled, but she didn't struggle; she floated on her back, and allowed me to pull her, my left hand under her chin, down to the shallow end of the pool where the water was less than three feet deep.

Her body was slick and cool; she bent her knees as she faced me, allowing her full breasts to bob and float on the surface for me to kiss—it was similar to the party game of bobbing for apples in a tub of water.

It was the first time that I had ever tried to make love in a swimming pool, and the problems were insurmountable. Gladys was willing enough; she was perfectly at home in the water. My passion would arise and then ebb away suddenly, and she would giggle as I pressed against her. Or she would lift her feet suddenly, hold her breath, and slide to the bottom of the pool unexpectedly.

At last, realizing the futility of my attempts, when she wouldn't cooperate with me, except in a passive manner, I gave up and swam over to the concrete steps that led down into the pool.

I sat on the top step, with just my feet and ankles in the water, and tried to breathe deeply without making any noise. The prolonged, one-sided struggle had made me weak, and the muscles of my legs were stiff and sore.

Gladys joined me, standing between my legs, with a hand on each of my knees for support. She wasn't fatigued; she wasn't even breathing hard—I had done all of the struggling.

"You hate her, don't you?" she whispered.

"Hate whom?" I replied, with genuine surprise.

"Your wife, of course." She sighed gently. "Didn't you know?"

"That's ridiculous," I said.

"Then why did you try to use me to get revenge?"

"Hate? Revenge? I don't know what you're talking about, for God's sake. Listen. There isn't a married man in the world who won't take advantage of a little strange poontang when it's available. And that's all there is to it, plain and simple."

"Are you sure, Richard?"

"I'm positive."

"Well…" She hesitated. "Perhaps I'm wrong. At least I prefer to think so. But remember one thing, Richard, I don't want to get involved. I'm a happily married woman."

The remark was incongruous, but she said it so seriously the thought of laughing didn't even occur to me. Besides, I was a happily married *man*—or at least I had been, up until this night.

"But if it's only sex…well, that's different, so long as we're very careful."

I put my hands on her shoulders, but she shrugged them away. "No, don't move," she whispered softly. "He can't see us—he's asleep." Slowly, very slowly, she slid her hands along my thighs, and wrapped her arms around my back as she knelt on the lower step. Her damp, thick, heavy hair cascaded over my face, and her tongue, hot and wet and caressing, moved avidly into my mouth.

"No, don't!" I whispered, looking apprehensively toward the closed bedroom window. I tried to push her away, but she merely tightened her arms behind my back. And then I was unable to stop her. I gripped her against the metal rails of the ladder so hard I could almost feel my fingerprints leaving their marks in the steel. My legs stiffened, shivering with an urgency of a passion I couldn't control, and I was completely submerged, drowned in a savage, primitive emotion. But even in the final moment of release, as the highly keyed tensions of my body drained away, and I sat there weak and shuddering, there was still enough emotion left over for me to feel sorry for Victor Chatham, who was sleeping away not twenty feet from the pool in the bedroom. I didn't feel sorry for him because I was taking advantage of his wife, but because he was a damned fool for not taking advantage of her himself.

Gladys backed away in the water, turned, and swam toward the deep end of the pool. I didn't follow her. I struggled to my feet, slipped into my shorts and my one shoe, and limped away as I had entered, through the Florida holly hedge.

It seemed as if several hours passed, but I was home for at

least an hour before Beryl arrived. When she entered the bedroom she stumbled slightly, and I knew she was more than a little tipsy. For a moment I pretended to be asleep. I faked a loud snore, and rolled over in bed as she turned on the light and lowered the blinds over the window. But she wasn't fooled, not for an instant.

She giggled foolishly, and as I watched her through my slitted, half-closed eyes, she hurriedly undressed, tossing items of apparel to the left and to the right in a haphazard manner, finally kicking off her shoes. I hadn't seen her so high in several years, but she wasn't so tight that she wouldn't want to make love. I didn't have a chance to get out of it, and I knew it. Early in our marriage we had made a solemn pact, and more than once the agreement had saved our partnership from near disasters. We had vowed that all disputes, fights, and arguments stopped at the bedroom door. A man and woman can never share the same bed if they both want all the covers.

Beryl came crawling toward me, a wicked smile on her lips; in spite of myself I had to laugh at the earnest expression on her face. The mixture of her perfume and the gin she had put away at the cast party was strong in my nostrils. Her kisses were so ardent and demanding I wondered for an ugly moment if she had been necking with someone at the party to be so stirred up—or if she had stopped somewhere for a round of heavy petting with whoever it was who had brought her home. This jealous thought was overwhelmed immediately by my own feeling of guilt and, besides I knew from past experience that it was the gin that loosened her inhibitions. I was still angry at Beryl about the play, but I wasn't mad at her body. I had had enough sex for one day, more than enough, and although I wanted to make love to Beryl I was worried for a moment about being able to do so—a needless worry. This was no loveless affair between two indifferent people; Beryl's warm soft mouth and tender passionate kisses came from her heart as well as her body.

All of her reactions and responses had been speeded up by the gin, and she couldn't have waited for me if she had wanted to, but for once I didn't care. It was the first time in months that I managed to beat her into the bathroom afterwards, and this small victory almost made up for the woman's traitorous action in taking a part in the play. *Almost*.

Chapter Eight

For breakfast the next morning I didn't have any.

Beryl's lips were poked out sullenly; her eyes glared venomously; and her back was stiff with rage. When I informed her that I was ready for my breakfast, she snarled, and told me to fix it myself. I shrugged and looked keenly at the woman, noting with inner satisfaction that her gray eyes were rimmed with old rose, the dark color of a cock's comb. A lovely, lovely hangover from the cast party. Too bad. Tough.

I poured a cup of coffee, but I had no intention of preparing my own breakfast. I knew how to fry eggs, bacon, and the operation of a toaster is a simple matter, but the husband who succumbs to such a temptation is lost forever. Beryl's sullen mood would pass, and within a day or so she would be fixing my breakfast again; so I wasn't going to set any loser's precedent by fixing my own meals.

As I glanced through the newspaper I couldn't fail to notice that a section of the movie-and-restaurant ads page had been ripped out. "If you're looking for your old review," Beryl said childishly, "you won't find it! I tore it out and burned it."

"That's all right, sweetie. I was only going to check it for possible typographical errors, and I can do that later at the office."

"Why did you do that to me?" she demanded, raising her voice. "I simply can't understand how you could be so vindictive!"

"Do what?" I said calmly, feigning astonishment.

"'Beryl Hudson was adequate in the role of Julie!'" she quoted bitterly from my review.

"Why, you were adequate, honey. What did you expect me to say? That you were mediocre? You really were mediocre, which is an excellent descriptive phrase. I didn't use it, however, because it has been misused so often that many people misconstrue mediocre to mean less than average. So I used adequate instead."

"Everybody at the party last night said I was wonderful! And I thought that you, for a change, would be proud of me…" Her lips trembled.

"Proud of you!" I said, wadding the newspaper and tossing it on the floor. "After you made a laughingstock out of me? What in the hell was the big idea in keeping the thing a secret?" I calmed down, lowering my voice. "Hell, sweetie, if you had only told me that you wanted to play the part, I'd have helped you with it, coached you in your lines—"

"No, you wouldn't." Beryl shook her head. "You'd only laugh at me. I know you too well, Richard Hudson. First, you would've tried to talk me out of it, making out that I was a damned fool. If that hadn't worked you would've made fun of me, and finally, I'd be so upset and nervous I'd have either quit or made a big failure out of the part. You won't believe me, I know, but I honestly didn't want to play Julie. The only reason I went to the tryouts in the first place was to have something to do in the evenings. And that's what I told Mr. Leanard. I told him I could help out with props and things backstage, but he insisted that I read for the part. When he gave it to me I was terrified and told him so. But he promised to help me and he did and—"

"Whose idea was it to keep it a secret? Yours or his?"

"It was mine. I discussed it with him, and when I told him how you'd carry on, he said if keeping the part a secret would help the show, he'd keep it a secret. That's why the publicity release to the paper said that Julie hadn't been cast yet."

"So you felt it necessary to discuss me with the director? I'm going to tell you something right now, little sister, and you'd better remember it! Your job around here is to be an adequate housewife, not an adequate actress. You don't even know how to speak, much less get up on the stage before a paying audience!"

"I'll fix your breakfast," Beryl said quietly, turning away. The familiar martyr bit.

"Never mind." I got up from the table. "I've got to go downtown. Where's your purse? I need five dollars."

"I'll get some money for you."

I finished dressing in the bedroom, and picked up the money Beryl had counted out on the dinette table. She had set up the ironing board, and was sprinkling clothes when I crossed to the front door. I took out my Zippo lighter, flicked it on, and held it up along the edge of the ceiling molding. There wasn't much smoke from the lighter, but little is needed to expose cobwebs. There were a few puffs of cobwebs on the ceiling and they turned black from the coil of smoke.

"Look," I said. "The house is being taken over by spiders while you trot around on the stage, neglecting your duties."

Beryl remained unperturbed; I had pulled the trick on her before. "I gave the house a thorough cleaning last Friday," she said coolly.

"Yes, but this is Thursday!" And on that triumphant note, I left the house and got into the car. It was just about time, I thought, for me to have a little talk with Mr. Jack Huneker.

On the drive to Huneker's brick and ornamental ironwork establishment, however, I wondered if I was being absolutely fair to my wife. There was room for doubt; at least she was acting as if there were, and it was possible that she really had thought I would be pleased. She wasn't too bright—a simple southern girl—but she was a better than average wife, all things considered. Whenever I wanted a clean shirt or a clean pair of socks or shorts, all I had to do was open the bureau drawer. Buddy was always neat and clean for school, and Beryl managed well on my slender salary. Every Saturday, without fail, I endorsed my paycheck and handed it over to her without a word. She did all of the buying, budgeting, and gave me a few dollars without question any time I asked for money. Of course, there wasn't any rent to pay, but she had to save up $500 for taxes every year, and she had bought $200 in savings bonds; and there were five or six hundred dollars in the savings account. Still, she should have come to me for permission to play Julie! I could have helped her with the part. For Beryl to say that I would have laughed at her was decidedly unfair. After nine years of marriage she should have known me better than that!

The skinny secretary in Huneker's outer office was a plain young woman with dun hair that looked as if she had cut it herself, and without using a mirror. She wore a shapeless blue linen dress that called attention to her muddy complexion. She was bent absorbedly over her typewriter and when I rapped on her desk for attention her big brown eyes widened in fright. There was a blue-black streak on her right cheek from carbon paper.

"I want to see Mr. Huneker. I'm Hudson, from the *News–Press*."

"Mr. Huneker isn't in right now. Would you care to leave a message?"

"No. When'll he be in?"

"I don't know…he's talking to Father Hardy…about the funeral!" She finished with a slight wail, and to my astonishment, followed the statement with tears. She recovered very quickly, and straightened herself in the posture typing chair.

"I'm sorry, Mr. Hudson," she apologized, grimacing, "but every time I think about it I get a little upset."

"Don't apologize. To cry is a woman's privilege, whether she has a reason or not, and I understand. You don't know when the boss'll be back then?"

"No, sir. He hasn't been in since—"

"Is Mr. O'Keeffe in the yard?"

"Yes, sir. He's—" She pointed through the glass back door, and would have given me directions, but I left abruptly. I knew the way. Although I had never met Huneker, I knew Red O'Keeffe, his foreman, almost too well.

Red O'Keeffe was the post commander of the local American Legion Post, and I saw him at the clubhouse almost every Sunday morning. When I finished dropping Beryl and Buddy off at the Unitarian Fellowship services on Sunday, I killed the time before picking them up again by drinking beer at the Legion clubhouse.

In addition to being a professional veteran—although Red had served but six months during World War II, and had never left the continental limits of the U.S.—O'Keeffe was a man filled with all kinds of delightful prejudices. It was always a pleasure to talk to him, just to find out what he was indignant about this time. And because I liked him, I had given him many column inches of publicity concerning Legion affairs in the newspaper, even though I wasn't a member myself. Red was tracing some intricate designs at a stand-up drawing board in his cluttered yard office when I tapped him on the shoulder.

"Hi, Red. I came down to see Huneker, but he wasn't in, so I thought I'd pay you a call."

"You doin' the story on his wife?" he said eagerly, wiping his big hands on the bib of his blue overalls. His red hair was peppered with gray, which made him look younger than he really was, somehow; his face looked as if he had washed it in tomato soup, particularly when he was sweating freely, and his face was always wet. Always.

I nodded. "I'm doing a sort of follow-up," I admitted.

"This tragedy's hit Jack mighty hard," Red said solemnly. "Marion was a funny girl in a lot of ways, Richard, but suicide, killing those fine kids—it's a mystery to me." He pursed his lips, and made a smacking noise.

"What do you mean she was funny?"

"The way she put on airs. That girl was too big for her britches, Richard. Me and my wife had dinner with 'em a few times, but she put on the dog too much, and after awhile, I plain out and told Jack not to ask me over anymore because I wasn't comin'. Two or three different kinds of wine with dinner, and that kind of crap! The first time we went over I was wearin' a sportshirt, just like everybody else in Florida. Why would anybody live in this hot, miserable state if they couldn't dress the way they wanted? And Jack pulled me off into the bedroom, made me put on one of his sport coats. 'Marion likes her guests to wear a coat at dinner,' he says. Oh, I went along with it, and the next couple of times I wore a coat when I was asked over, and then, like I said, I quit goin'. Poor old Jack, she had him dressed up in a coat and tie every damned night, even when it was eighty-five and ninety. Course, their house's air-conditioned, but even so…Jack's okay, don't get me wrong. He just got stuck with the wrong woman, that's all."

"The paper makes us wear a coat and tie, too. You get used to it, Red, but you don't like it."

"If I was you, I'd quit, by God!" He mopped his face with a red bandana.

"Would you give me a job?" I grinned.

"Startin' now! And no matter what you're makin' I'll raise it five bucks a week to start. All I got now are a bunch of shiftless niggers. One of 'em come up to me last week and asked me, big's you please, mind you, what was the company plannin' in way of a pension plan! I paid him off right then. 'Here's your pension, boy,' I told him. 'Now git!'" Red chuckled richly.

"I knew there was some reason I didn't want to work for you, Red." I grinned. "No pension plan."

Red laughed again, and pounded me on the shoulder. "I guess you better stay on the paper at that!" he said, wiping his face again.

Because I was curious I mentioned the incident in the office, telling Red about the secretary bursting into tears.

"She's got reasons," he smiled broadly. "Yes, she's got her reasons."

"Evidently," I said casually, "she thought quite a bit of the late Mrs. Huneker."

"You're wrong, Richard." Red looked around, went to the doorway and surveyed the yard, and then nodded. "This is just between me and you and the lamppost, but Helen—Helen Devereaux's her name—was sleepin' with Jack Huneker on the side." He lowered his voice to a coarse, confidential whisper. "Seems like Marion had cut him off at home, so he was getting a little overtime out of the secretary." He winked. "Fact is, Richard, I put Jack onto her myself. You know how it is; every married man likes a little strange stuff now and then. But after I wised Jack up to Helen, I was out in the cold!" He chuckled deep in his throat. "Helen got the wild idea somewhere that Jack'd divorce Marion, and then she'd get him. See the picture?"

"I wonder," I said, probingly, "if Mrs. Huneker found out about the affair. That could've been her motive for suicide."

"Not a chance." Bill shook his head. "Jack told Marion all about Helen one night when he was drunk. Marion was just

happy he had a girl someplace and wasn't bothering her any-
more, that's all. There's a lot of women like that, Richard. But
Helen was living in a dream—Jack would no more have divorced
Marion than I would Lottie."

"Why the tears then? Huneker's a widower, and the field is
open, isn't it?"

"Use your head, Richard." Red said with exasperation. "When
a man gets married he wants a decent girl, not some tramp
who's sleepin' around. If a woman'll sleep with a man before
she's married to him she'll sleep with another after she's married. That's a fact. While Jack was married Helen could kid herself into thinkin' that some day he'd get a divorce, but now that
he hasn't got a wife anymore, the dream is over. See how that
is?"

"Damned strange reasoning, if you ask me, Red."

"You just don't know women the way I do, Richard. I imagine
Helen's worried now 'cause she thinks Jack'll fire her. And I
guess he will, too. Not much else he can do, the way I see it."

"I suppose you're right, Red. She could get pregnant or
something, and trap him easily now."

"Well, Jack won't fire her; I'll have to do it, and I'm a tender-
hearted guy. But Jack won't fire anybody. About six months
ago, one of the ironworkers got drunk on the weekend and
broke his leg. You won't believe this, Richard, but Jack kept on
payin' his salary for two months until he could get back to work.
He didn't have to, and I told him he didn't have to, but that's
the kind of guy he is."

"I'm getting anxious to meet Mr. Huneker," I said.

"He's got a stubborn streak in him, though. Suicides don't
get any Requiem Mass, and they aren't buried in consecrated
ground. But Jack's got his mind made up to have Marion and
the kids buried together, and when he makes up his mind,

that's that. Him and Father Hardy are going 'round and 'round right now, but my dough's on Jack Huneker!"

"You'll lose, Red. There are some things—"

"Just wait and see."

"I've got to get going, Red. It would probably be better if I waited until after the funeral to talk to Mr. Huneker anyway."

Red shook his head, and broadened his smile. "Don't make any difference when you see him, Richard. He ain't goin' to tell you anything."

"Why won't he?"

"He'll tell you it's none of your business."

"As a newspaperman," I said hotly, "everything is my business."

"You tell Jack that, and you'll end with a black eye." Chuckling, mopping futilely at his red face, O'Keeffe bent over his drawings, and I left his ratty little office.

I paused for a moment in front of the secretary's desk to light a cigarette and to take another surreptitious look at the office siren. I was truly amazed; I couldn't see how any man could work up any desire for this bony little girl. While I had been out in the back, talking to Red, Helen Devereaux had touched up her lips with purple lipstick, and powdered her face, but these touches of make-up made her look worse. When a man had had a good-looking woman like Marion Huneker at home, it just wasn't reasonable to have an affair with a girl like this secretary. The only plausible explanation was that Helen was available, and his wife wasn't; and every time he had passed the girl's desk, there she was, waiting. One day, on an impulse, he must have driven her home after work or taken her to dinner, and the affair had begun...

"Did you find Mr. O'Keeffe all right?" Helen asked brightly, feeling my eyes upon her.

"Yes, thanks. Just take a short message for Mr. Huneker, and tell him I'll try and catch him later on this week at his home."

"Yes, sir. I'll tell him."

For a few minutes I sat in my car, wondering what to do next. So far, my knowledge concerning Marion Huneker added up to zero, although I thought I detected a pattern of some kind. Maybe her priest could divulge something; as her confessor he knew more about the dead woman than any person alive. As I drove to the Church of the Sacred Heart I thought how easy my assignment would be if I only had tape recordings of the last three or four confessions she had made to the old priest.

Chapter Nine

As Roman Catholic churches go, the Church of the Sacred Heart wasn't large, but it had a wealthy membership. The percentage of Roman Catholics in Lake Springs was approximately eleven percent, and those who attended Mass were forced to go to the Church of the Sacred Heart because it was the only Catholic church in town.

After parking in the yellow loading zone in front of the church I went inside, and soon spotted Father Hardy down by the altar doing something or other with a stand of candelabra. There were two teenaged girls kneeling together, midway down the aisle, their heads covered with pink Kleenex cleansing tissues, but except for the girls and the old priest, the church was empty. I lit a cigarette and sat down in the last row of pews to wait for Father Hardy. The high-ceilinged church was cool, and it was a quiet, restful place to relax in. The multicolored stained glass windows along both walls were beautiful to contemplate, and gave the interior an aura of mystery. How nice it would be, I thought, to truly have faith in a religion like this, where a man could take his problems to God, through the medium of an understanding priest, and be forgiven for his sins—that is, if he had any. But the Mother Church hadn't helped Marion Huneker when she had sorely needed it. Why?

Father Hardy came puffing up the aisle, white-haired, pink-cheeked, his enormous paunch hiking his black cassock up six inches higher in front than it was in the back. A muskmelon can be majestic, but it cannot be dignified, no matter how hard it tries. Smiling and shaking his round head, the priest wagged an authoritative finger.

"No smoking in church," he said firmly.

"Why not?" I said, getting to my feet and falling in beside him. "Would God be offended?"

"No," he said gently, with a sidewise look, "but the Fire Marshal wouldn't like it."

We paused outside, at the top of the steps, both of us blinking in the bright sunlight. I tossed my cigarette onto the verdant, well-kept yard, in the general direction of a "Keep Your Dogs Off The Lawn" sign.

"I'd like to talk to you for a few minutes about Mrs. Huneker, Father. I'm Richard Hudson, from the *News–Press*."

"Of course. I've just been talking to her husband." Father Hardy sighed gently, shaking his head. "And I lit a candle for the poor woman."

"How much did the candle cost Mr. Huneker?"

"Twenty dollars," the old priest snapped without hesitation. "Let's go to the house where we can sit down in the shade." He took my arm and we went next door to his two-story house. After righting two upturned aluminum patio chairs we sat down on the wide front porch. "It's such a hot day, you might like a glass of lemonade, Mr. Hudson?"

"No, thanks. I know you're a busy man, and I don't want to take up too much of your time, Father. I'm doing the follow-up story on the murder–suicide story, and rumor has it that Mrs. Huneker and her children will all be buried in the same plot of ground. This isn't the ordinary practice, is it, for suicides?"

"Rumors travel quickly in Lake Springs." Father Hardy looked at me with mild surprise. "Mr. Huneker left me less than ten minutes ago." He examined his fingernails for a moment; they were cleanly pared, and shiny from a coat of clear lacquer.

"Ordinarily," he continued in a level, matter-of-fact tone of voice, "suicides are not buried in our Calvary Cemetery, not unless there are extenuating circumstances. But in this particular case there were such circumstances. Mrs. Huneker was mentally ill."

"Every person who takes his own life is mentally ill, in one way or another, or don't you agree?"

"I agree to some extent, yes. But each case is different, and must be handled separately. A Requiem Mass will be offered for Mrs. Huneker, and her children, of course, tomorrow morning. There are no doubts whatsoever that Mrs. Huneker was mentally disturbed. Several years ago, when the couple was living in Pennsylvania, Mrs. Huneker was treated for a nervous breakdown. Mr. Huneker showed me some of the bills that he had retained from the psychiatrist who had treated his wife—"

"It was fortunate he kept them. What was the diagnosis?"

"There wasn't any exact diganosis; it was a nervous condition of some kind that affected her scalp. Her illness began, Mr. Huneker told me, with a violent scalp rash she couldn't get rid of. The family practitioner recommended a psychiatrist. And any rate, after a few psychiatric consultations the rash disappeared, and she didn't make any more visits. It's a pity she didn't continue them. The underlying causes of the nervous condition she suffered may have been uncovered completely had she—"

"I don't know, Father," I interrupted, with a little laugh, "and it isn't any of my business, but that sounds like mighty slim evidence for mental illness."

"Illness may be the incorrect term to describe the case, Mr. Hudson. The Catholic Church regards suicide as a sin, a grievous sin, and doesn't, by any means, condone Mrs. Huneker's actions. However, she was definitely, in my considered opinion, mentally *irresponsible* at the time. When a reasonable, solid doubt exists, as it does here, the Church is merciful. Eternity is a long time, Mr. Hudson, and I knew the poor woman well. She was a good mother, and I cannot impute willfulness to this tragedy."

"I suppose you checked your decision with the Bishop of Miami?"

Father Hardy closed his eyes, smiled, and slowly shook his head. "I was ordained in 1927, Mr. Hudson, and my superiors have confidence in my judgment in such matters."

"I see. So mother, son, and daughter will be buried together tomorrow?"

"Yes. Calvary Cemetery, two o'clock. And please, no photographs."

"Of course. One more thing, Padre. It has been estimated that Mr. Huneker averages about thirty thousand dollars a year in earnings. Does he give ten percent of this income, or three thousand dollars a year, to the Church of the Sacred Heart?"

"What is your faith, Mr. Hudson?"

"Zen Buddhism." I grinned. "But I don't practice it because there aren't any Zen Masters living in Lake Springs at present."

"In other words, none?"

"That's right, Father. None. And please excuse my stupid facetiousness. A man should never scoff at what he doesn't understand. I'm just an ignorant sinner, I guess, and I apologize."

"Newspapermen have a tendency to carry their skepticism as a shield. Perhaps, one day, you and I can have a little talk?"

"Perhaps. I realize that the confessional is a deep, dark secret, Father Hardy, but are you allowed to tell me about the last time Mrs. Huneker came to you and confessed?"

"Do you rub everybody the wrong way, Mr. Hudson? Or am I overly sensitive?" The priest heaved himself out of the chair, leaned against the rail of the porch and studied my face. "I believe," he said, nodding with conviction, "that you are a very rude, unpleasant, young man."

"I think I am, too," I agreed. "But if I don't ask questions I don't get any answers."

"Your last question wasn't germane. Anything else? I have a crowded schedule, Mr. Hudson."

"Yes, sir. I'd like to have a list of the pallbearers, if you have it. Names make news, you know."

"All right. The list isn't completed, as yet. But I'll telephone the names to your paper when I have them all."

"Make it early, Father. My deadline is eleven-forty-five tonight."

"That's your problem, not mine!" he snapped. "I'll call the paper when I have them. No! On second thought, you can call the Ivy Street Funeral Home and get them yourself."

"Thanks." I got out of the chair. "And if you have the name and address of the Pennsylvania psychiatrist, I'd like to have it. It might be 'germane' to drop him a line and see what his diagnosis was."

"Good day, Mr. Hudson," he said coldly.

"Good day, Padre."

The priest ignored my outstretched hand and marched into his house. Overly sensitive, Father Hardy.

Sitting in my car I made some notes for a story about the funeral before driving downtown and parking in the newspaper lot. I had a bowl of soup and a pimento cheese sandwich in Frank's Lunchroom. Then I walked three blocks to the public library to kill a couple of hours until it was time to report to the office for work.

The old biddy behind the desk gave me a tight-lipped, suspicious expression along with the key to the glass case where the medical books were kept locked away from the prying eyes of the junior and senior high school students. The library board was afraid that these young students, who used the library for study purposes at night, might possibly learn the differences between male and female by looking at the pictures. One of the books even went so far as to explain all about babies, with diagrams in full color.

I picked out several thick texts, and did some general reading on paresis and dermatology. The meager information I had obtained from the good priest was insufficient to fit Mrs. Huneker into any of the case histories I found in the small print. If she had made only a few visits to a psychiatrist, and had been so easily cured of a so-called psychosomatic rash, I decided she couldn't have been seriously disturbed emotionally. The kind-hearted old priest was clutching at straws; more power to the old boy, and God bless him.

The gobbledygook in the psychiatry textbooks made interesting reading, however, and I made a great many notes for statistic tables I could prepare later to mystify my readers. The causes of psychoneuroses were explained in detail, and if anything, Mrs. Huneker had been a psychoneurotic. But weren't we all?

The causes: Sexual disturbances, 22 percent; Accidents, with or without injury, 13 percent; Marital crises, 12 percent; Financial crises, 11 percent; Operations, 10 percent; and Deaths or illnesses in the family, 9 percent each. Other contributing factors included an unfavorable early home life, constitutional predisposition, the menopause, scars, anxiety, physical defects, and as a kind of catchall, overconcern about any of the symptoms the person complained about!

As a layman attempting to figure out something I didn't know anything about, I was forced to the conclusion that everybody I knew, myself included, had psychoneurotic tendencies, and that all of us were logical candidates for suicide. But I had known that much before I had started reading... I locked the books up again, returned the key to the desk, and went to the office.

My compatriot, Dave Finney, looked up from his typewriter, checked his wristwatch, and clucked his tongue. "You're slipping, Richard. Twenty minutes early."

"I know, but stuff is beginning to stack up on me."

"More than you know!" He laughed cheerfully. "You're Mrs. Frances Worthington this week!"

"For once you're wrong, Dave. I checked the schedule Monday."

"And I rechecked it this morning. I know that Mrs. Mosby never makes a mistake, but this time she transposed our names when she typed the list."

"Are you sure?"

"Positive; I'm not kidding you, Richard. But the tough part's already done. Rex and I took the photos already, and we got six or seven fairly good eight-by-tens. There's a note on top of the pics for you." He patted the stack of photos on the desk.

"Okay, okay," I said wearily. "I'm Mrs. Worthington."

"How's the suicide business?"

"Not so good, Dave. It's a painful conundrum, a painful conundrum indeed." I sat down, pulled on my lower lip. "That might make a fair title for the series; A Painful Conundrum—"

Dave giggled. "You can't get away with it, Richard! Dickens, or maybe Conan Doyle might have been able to use that title, but our readers would think you were referring to a tight condom!"

"It's a sad situation," I agreed, grinning, "but you're probably right."

While Dave cleared up the desk I went into the morgue to get the stack of old *House Beautiful* and *Living For Young*

Homemakers magazines I used for research purposes when I was Mrs. Worthington. I plopped the magazines down on the desk, and took a look at Dave's note. The featured house of the week belonged to a retired couple from Duluth. They had a son in college and a married daughter in Cincinnati. As usual, the address was a good one, and the photos revealed that their home was on the lake, so it was expensive.

"Tell me something, Richard," Dave said earnestly, as I sat down in the still-warm vacated swivel chair behind the desk. "How in the hell can you write these Mrs. Worthington features without talking to the homeowners or visiting the sites?"

"Experience, my boy, experience, but it's a secret for you and me to share, and not for J.C.'s ears. Don't ever mention it to him; it would break our M.E.'s heart."

"Either you're crazy or lazy."

"I'm both, and that isn't a secret."

Dave departed, and I made some notes for the evening's work ahead. I was forced to cancel my attendance at the Jaycees' banquet, and to call the secretary and ask him to drop by the office afterwards with his minutes on the affair. There was the general outline for the series on suicide I had to get out of the way. Four separate articles would do it; the first a general piece on suicide, and I had enough for that one already. I could always fill in, if I ran short, with information from the *World Almanac* and the office *Americana Encyclopedia*. The second article would be an exposition on female suicide; the third on male; and the fourth and final piece: suicide–murder, adolescent self-destruction and perhaps a summation. A fine plan of action, and if I was lucky Mr. Curtis would pay me a hundred dollars. It would be extra money and Beryl could use it to buy herself a couple of dresses and some new shoes or something.

I had plenty of work to do without being stuck as Mrs.

Worthington, I thought disgustedly. I detested the unexpected assignment.

Every Sunday the paper ran a lead feature article on a Lake Springs residence in the Home and Real Estate Section. In addition to several photos of the outside and inside layout, the descriptive phrases describing the home were written in a gushy manner. The three female writers on the editorial staff did the best job on this kind of article, but because everybody disliked the task, J.C. had compromised by rotating the assignment to a different reporter every week—except for the two sports reporters. He didn't consider them capable of such writing. This was a sore point with me, because both sportswriters were paid ten dollars a week more than me. In reality, there was no such person as Mrs. Frances Worthington, and there never had been. The pen name was used from the beginning of the feature because no one on the paper wanted to be identified with the articles. When publicity-seeking readers called the paper, anxious to make a pitch to the nonexistent Mrs. Worthington to get their homes featured, they were given a standard answer: "Mrs. Worthington is attending the National Home Conference in St. Louis. We'll see that she gets your message when she returns."

My phone rang. The phone rang all the time. Sometimes I answered it and sometimes I didn't. If I was in the middle of something I left the receiver off the stand. This time I answered the summons.

"Richard, this is Gladys."

"Gladys who?"

"Gladys Chatham."

"Oh, yes. What can I do for you, Mrs. Chatham?"

"I was wondering if you and your wife could come over to our house for dinner one night next week—after the play is over?"

"Sorry, Gladys. But I'm working every night."

"How about cocktails, then? Sunday evening."

"Where'll I meet you?"

"I mean you and your wife. She appears to me like a person I'd like to meet and know."

"How come this sudden, unnatural interest in my wife?"

"Because I feel sorry for her, that's why!" Gladys said angrily. "I read your review of *Lilliom* this morning and I think you treated her shabbily. Adequate! She was marvelous in the role and you know it!"

"I'm glad you think so. I'll tell Beryl. She'll be pleased."

"If you were my husband, which thank God you're not, and you wrote about me like that, I'd slap you every way but loose!"

"If I may be so bold as to express an opinion, I think I wrote an excellent review. If you don't agree with me, and that's a reader's privilege, why don't you write an angry letter to the editor?"

"I may do that!"

"Good. I'll enjoy reading it before I tear it up."

"You're no good, Richard, just plain out and out no good!"

"I'm busy, Mrs. Chatham. Is there anything else on your mind?"

If I hadn't been prudent enough to hold the receiver away from my ear I might have received a punctured eardrum. Gladys slammed the phone down very hard indeed. I laughed, the familiar, ugly snuffling sound through my nose. But there wasn't anything funny, nothing to laugh about. The quick fury in Gladys' voice was not feigned. She was angry all right, but why? She didn't know Beryl; why should she feel called upon to defend her? She didn't even know me for that matter. And that was the true answer. Gladys had suffered an attack of remorse, and she had decided that she didn't want to know me. The column had given her an excuse to relieve her guilty conscience; to nip our embryonic affair in the bud before it went any farther. Fine. In a few days, however, her boredom would probably overcome her temporary guilt and she'd call me again—to kiss and make up. Tough. I was through. The excuse worked both ways, and I made up my mind to be as impersonal as the weather if she ever called me again.

The phone rang, and I grabbed it.

"I found that shoe you lost in my hedge," Gladys announced. "I'll mail it to you!" This time she was too quick for me—the phone slammed down at the other end, and my ear rang for at least an hour. No matter.

Whistling, relieved that the affair had ended so easily for us both, I inserted a piece of yellow copy paper in the typewriter and went to work...

Chapter Ten

Friday morning at ten-thirty, when I got out of bed, my wife and the car were missing. Beryl had left a note for me on the dinette table stating that she *simply had to do some shopping*, and that if I wasn't home when she returned she would park the car for me at the newspaper lot after three-thirty and take the bus home. This was a standard operating procedure we had followed many times.

With a legitimate excuse I prepared my own breakfast, and instead of an argument or a strained silence I had an excellent, leisurely meal. Reading the paper I noted with a small degree of triumph that the M.E. had allowed my short item concerning the priest's interpretation of the Roman Catholic rules about suicide to stand without any editing.

The house was quiet, the way I thought I liked it to be, but I was unable to do any constructive thinking about my play. I spent almost an hour scotchtaping the torn pages together again. Neither Beryl nor Buddy was allowed in my study without an invitation, and the room was usually dirty unless I cleaned it myself. Dusting, sweeping, and mopping consumed another forty minutes. The mail came: a letter from Beryl's mother in Gainesville which I didn't open, and a bill from the Don-Lawn Spray Company which I did. The lawn had been sprayed for chinch bugs—$15.00! I wrote a memo and paper-clipped it to the bill. *Are we rich? R.* I put the bill and Beryl's letter on the dinette table, and took a shower, preparatory to getting dressed for town.

At three that afternoon, my coat draped over my arm, I entered Dr. Maxwell Goldman's air-conditioned clinic. My mood was foul. I had missed the bus, and rather than wait twenty minutes in the hot sun for the next one, I had walked all the way to the clinic. The three-mile walk, in the humid, eighty-degree temperature, had been a mistake. My hair, my face, and my fresh white shirt were soaking wet with perspiration.

Three patient tumescent women, each with a fruit jar of urine clasped in their laps, occupied tangerine Eames chairs along the terra-cotta wall. I looked at them curiously and they stared back; resentfully, I thought. The middle-aged nurse got up from behind her desk as I approached. Through her white, transparent nylon uniform I could count four straps looping over each shoulder. I was puzzled. A slip and a brassiere could account for two sets, but the other two? All I could do was guess, and I decided she wore three slips instead of one, to make certain that no one could see a portion of her trunk through her transparent uniform.

"Do you have an appointment with Dr. Goldman?" The nurse said, sternly, efficiently.

"No. If I had an appointment I'd be carrying a full fruit jar just like everybody else. Just inform Dr. Goldman that Mr. Hudson wants to see him."

She flushed easily, and jerked her head sharply to the right. "If you care to make an appointment, Mr. Hudson, I'll see what dates I have open." She turned the sheets of an open ledger on her desk.

"Never mind, nurse, I'll see him now."

"I'm afraid that's impossible," she said happily.

"I'm from the *News-Press*." I showed her the press card in my wallet but she was unimpressed,

"If you want an appointment, Mr. Hudson," she said doggedly, "I may be able to squeeze you in three weeks from today."

A young girl came out of the doctor's inner sanctum—she didn't look pregnant to me—and opened a small red purse at the nurse's desk.

"Is the doctor free now, little lady?" I smiled pleasantly.

"Yes, sir," she replied timidly. "I mean, I'm all through 'til next Friday week."

I started for the door and the nurse snagged my arm with her claws. "I said you'd have to make an appointment, Mr. Hudson!"

"Get your clammy hand off my arm!" I told her fiercely. I entered the doctor's office and closed the door behind me. The nurse didn't try to follow me inside, but her voice came in loud and clear through the intercom on the doctor's desk.

"That's all right," he said calmly, "I'll talk to him." He hit the switch on the gray box, cutting her off in midsentence. "Well, you're in to see me," the doctor said briskly. "What do you want?"

I didn't know; I hadn't thought that far ahead. To stall for time I lit a cigarette I didn't want to smoke. Dr. Goldman wore a white three-quarter length jacket, so he looked like a doctor. Except for an iron-gray tonsure encircling his tanned head, he was bald, and his curving nose was pocked with deep, large pores. He was a slender man, but his hands looked strong and capable.

"I'm sorry to intrude this way, Doctor," I apologized. "I'm Hudson, from the newspaper, and I'm working on a story. A three-week wait for an appointment seemed a bit too long."

"Go on. I have patients waiting," he said grimly.

"The late Mrs. Huneker was one of your patients. And I'd like to have—"

"I've already informed one of your reporters over the phone that I have no comments concerning Mrs. Huneker."

"I know you did, and that's why I'm here. If you have no comment that means you're covering up something. What is it?"

"I'm not covering up anything," he barked. "There isn't anything to tell."

"Then you shouldn't mind answering a few questions."

"But I do, and particularly at this time. I'm very busy now. If you have some questions, put them in writing and mail them to me. And when I have time I'll answer those I consider ethical."

"All I want to know is whether Mrs. Huneker was pregnant?"

"No. No she was not."

"Could she have had any children? That is, if she wanted to?"

"I told you I was busy. I must ask you to leave."

Through an open door behind the doctor's desk I could see a brown leather examining table, the kind that has stirrups to hold a woman's feet when her legs are spread. I lifted my chin. "You had Mrs. Huneker on your table in there a few times, I suppose, with her feet in the stirrups?"

"Get out. Get out of my office." The doctor had his voice nicely under control but I could sense his inner fury.

"I've often wondered about gynecologists. Why would any man go into a dirty business like this?"

Dr. Goldman clicked the switch on the intercom. "Clara," he said, "get me the publisher of the *News-Press* on the phone."

"Tell her to call long distance. The publisher lives on Long Island, in New York," I suggested.

"Make that the managing editor, Clara," the doctor amended.

There was no point in remaining; I had managed to antagonize the man. I left his office and closed the door. The nurse was pawing through the telephone book, so I gave her the newspaper office number, to make it easier for her, before going outside.

The clinic was a low, white, brick building in the center of a black asphalt sea. I hadn't been inside long enough to cool off, but I had caught my breath in there. After coming out of the air-conditioning the sun seemed twice as hot. I tried to puzzle out my anger at the doctor—there didn't seem to be any good reason for it—and then I recalled the time some six months before when Beryl had had a bad cold and had gone to see Dr. Robertson. He was a man in his early thirties, and Beryl hadn't been in his office five minutes before he had her stripped from the waist down and on the table with her feet in the stirrups. When she told me about it later I had wanted to go down to Robertson's office and break his jaw for him. He had no excuse whatsoever to give her a pelvic examination; she'd only had a cold, for Christ's sake! She had talked me out of going to his office, but I had avoided him after that. As a father I had to admit that gynecologists and obstetricians were useful, but as a husband and lover I couldn't help resenting them. But my original distrust of obstetricians stemmed from before our marriage. After all, they would be out of pocket if it weren't for babies, and they conspired against young couples, married and unmarried, playing on their ignorance about such matters to get young girls pregnant as soon as it was humanly possible. Or so it had worked with Beryl.

In fact, the idea of getting married was not even a remote idea in my mind when I was dating Beryl at college. I had carnal designs on her, and that was as far as my thinking went. But night after night I was getting nowhere. I got close, but unlike horseshoes, I seemed to be playing a losing game. She would neck, up to a point, but she always kept her legs crossed. And she had a ridiculous rule about playing with her breasts. She would take out either the left or the right, but never both at the same time; one had to stay in the brassiere pocket at all times.

"In case somebody comes snooping around," she said, "it'll only take a sec to put one back."

Inasmuch as these necking and groping sessions were always in the front seat of my car, I couldn't argue the point with her, but I wasn't getting anywhere with her either. After a prolonged petting match that led nowhere I broke away from her, and hunched glumly over the steering wheel to watch the movie for awhile. We were at the drive-in, as usual, and again, as usual, the sound was switched off on the little speaker that rested on the car window. Some actor's lips were moving a mile-a-minute on the screen as he talked to Janet Leigh, but I had a hunch that he wasn't getting anywhere with her either.

In my mind I ran over the arguments I had used to no avail with Beryl already, searching my mind for a fresh approach. One argument, which I had marked off my list forever, was the one where the atom bomb is brought up—"Any day now the bomb is liable to be dropped, so why should we wait under such circumstances—life is so short—we only have the security of insecurity," etc. This line of reasoning had only made Beryl hysterical with laughter. But I was all out of fresh ideas, and when dating a campus beauty, who had been equally as pretty in high school, a fresh approach, or a new line is almost impossible to devise. She had heard them all, each and every one of them. And then I thought of one:

"Beryl," I said, "have you taken the course yet called Marriage and the Family, the one referred to as Sex 203?"

"No, not yet, but they say it's a snap course."

"It is, but there's an interesting statistic I learned in this course. Did you know that sixty percent of the married couples in the United States indulged in pre-marital intercourse?"

"That many?"

"That many. So when you refuse me, turn me down cold this way, you're only cheating yourself out of a practice that's commonplace. That's all. Do you see what I mean?" The silent lips on the giant screen flapped away, and I wondered how he was making out—

"That's different," Beryl said quietly, in a high, small voice. "You never said anything about 'pre-marital' before, Richard. I knew you liked me, and all, and I've been expecting you to propose right along—although I thought it'd be more romantic. I know that all the girls who are engaged—well, they don't wait, and it's the expected thing. So in that case…all right."

It took a couple of moments for the purport of her roundabout acquiescence to sink in, and I was more than a little bewildered by the unexpected turn my suggestions had taken. I hadn't proposed! The idea of proposing hadn't even entered my mind; she'd twisted it all around. Was she stupid or was she diabolically clever? But I wasn't thinking clearly; all I could think about was the fact that she had calmly said, "All right." And I suppose that acceptance, after nights and weeks of futile struggling and arguing, outweighed any and all thoughts about the fact that I would be engaged, committed to marry her following the act itself. But what did being engaged mean? It was nothing; many are called, but few are chosen, and I could get out of the marriage when the time came. The important thing was right now.

I reached for her, and was met by a stiff arm holding me at arm's length. "No," she said firmly.

"But you just said—" I began huffily.

"I said, 'All right,' and I meant it. But not here, in this place, on the front seat of your car like two animals. It isn't right, and you know it."

I turned on the car engine, put the speaker back on the rack with my left hand as I turned toward her. "You name it. We'll go anywhere you say, and right now."

"No," she shook her head. "Not now, not tonight, right after proposing. Wait till Saturday; that's only four days, but it'll give you time to think it over, to cool off. And then, if you still want to be engaged, we can go away for the weekend. To Jacksonville, or Valdosta, somewhere where we can go to a hotel or a motel. And besides, I don't want to get pregnant; and I'll have to buy a diaphragm."

"You don't have to do that. I can use a safety."

"No. Men don't like that. My doctor told me so when I talked to him about sex one afternoon when I was still in high school. We'll either do it right, and my way, or not at all."

"We'll do it your way."

I drove her home, and her neat, orderly mind formulated plans on the way. She would tell her parents she was going to spend the weekend with her girl friend in Orlando, so I'd have to pick her up at the Student Center, not at her home, etc.

I agreed with her all the way. And when I kissed her good night, the promise was implicit in her soft lips.

"I love you, Beryl," I said, and it was the first time I had ever said it—and I did. "Will you be at the Center Saturday?"

"I'll be there. Will you?"

"Of course. You don't have to test me—I'm ready to leave right now."

"We've both got classes tomorrow," she said practically, and she got out of the car.

I drove back to the dorm, and stumbled across the parking lot, with aching stones. And looking back, I must admit that she was fair. Four days were plenty to change my mind, and I wavered several times before Saturday rolled around, but there was never any real doubt in my mind that I'd meet her when the time came. On the contrary, I thought that she would change her mind—and when this thought occurred to me it would almost drive me mad with rage. Those four days were an eternity to me. I sat deaf, dumb, and blind through every lecture.

Saturday morning I was awake at five-thirty A.M. Before noon, I took three showers, and changed clothes as many times, deciding finally to wear my best suit, a black mohair job. I also borrowed a pair of pajamas from my roommate. I had none of my own, and his were too small for me, but I thought it would look more respectable that way, to lay out a pair of pajamas for the sake of appearances when we checked into a motel. I either slept raw or in my underwear, but she could find out about that later. In the back of my skull, however, I was already thinking of ways to break our engagement, or to pick a bitter quarrel—afterwards. But the "afterwards" might be over an extended period of time; this possibility didn't escape me. If it turned out that I had a good thing here, I could play her along for several months before breaking things off sharply. After all, an engagement wasn't anything tangible, like a date set for the marriage. The time to break up would be when she began to push for a certain date; then she'd find out that I didn't push so easily.

I got to the Student Center on-campus at eleven A.M., and she was there, so beautiful a hard lump leaped into my throat. She wore a white dress, and with her long black hair hanging down her back; and with the sweet Mary Jane shoes she was wearing, she reminded me of Alice, the Alice of Wonderland. She didn't look much more than sixteen or seventeen, and I began to worry about whether I could pass her off as a wife when I checked into a motel. I held open the door for her—another first for me—and tossed her bag into the back seat.

She sat demurely, looking straight ahead, with her hands folded in her lap. "I'm glad you came early, Richard," she said. "I had to come early, because I couldn't wait at home any longer."

"Didn't you expect me?"

"Well—yes, and then again, no!"

We both laughed then, and the tension was broken between us. It was a beautiful day, and at that moment I realized what a wonderful day it really was. I had never been any happier before in my entire life—and I marked everything in my mind, knowing that such days would be rare in the future—the way she looked, smelled, smiled, the color of her fresh, young skin, and even the clean, white, half-moon scar on her knee.

I had no real plan, and not much money. I had borrowed seven dollars, and I had sold my second-hand typewriter for eighteen more, and that was all. Valdosta was an ideal city for the purpose, and I had driven five miles up the highway before I realized that I would have to cross the state line into Georgia—which meant a violation of the Mann Act. At the next dirt road I turned in, and backed around.

"We'd better not go to Valdosta, honey," I said, "I used to play golf at the country club there when I was on the Golf Team, and too many people up there know me by name. Let's go to Daytona Beach instead. It's farther, but we can go swimming in the morning. All right?"

"I don't care."

"And besides," I added, "you look so young, it'll be better if we check in after dark. You can sit in the car, and—"

"Oh, I thought of that!" she said brightly, opening her purse. "I got my aunt's driver's license out of her purse, and all you have to do is sign the register with her husband's name. Howard Sibley. And if they say anything about me, I can show them the license—"

"How old is your aunt?"

She looked at the license. "*Thirty-seven!*" She said this with a cry of shocked dismay, and this incongruous age, which Beryl had failed to think about, kept us giggling and bursting out with fresh peals of laughter for fully twenty-five miles.

We needn't have worried. I stopped at a good motel that boasted of a swimming pool, and the main concern of the clerk was to get his twelve dollars in advance. He didn't even look at Beryl, who had remained in the car; he merely handed me the key, and pointed out the window. "Number eight. Count down eight cottages, and park your car in the space marked Eight."

I had a fifth of rum a friend had given me on his return from a weekend in the Bahamas, and the first thing I did was to fix us a drink; half-rum, and half-water from the tap. I figured we needed a drink. We were both shy again, now that we were alone in the motel room. And the double-bed seemed to occupy all of the existing space, in our minds, and in our room.

"I think I'll take a shower," I said at last, putting down my empty glass. "Or—maybe you'd like to take yours first?"

"Oh, no! Go ahead!"

I took my shaving kit, my robe, and the pajamas out of the bag, and entered the bathroom. And as I recall, I was so nervous I even locked the door. A second shave wasn't needed, but I shaved my face again anyway. I showered, and after drying off, plastered almost half of a tube of deodorant paste under my arms. Well brainwashed by advertising, I dreaded the thought of "offending" this sweet young girl with the honest male odor of acrid sweat.

And then it was Beryl's turn. I put the pajamas back into the suitcase, and paced the room as the shower ran on and on, interminably, it seemed. I smoked a cigarette, and then another. I fixed another drink, a big hooker, which I downed straight because I had failed to put any water in the pitcher. The shower had stopped a long time before—but still no Beryl.

I waited. I smoked another cigarette. I checked my watch, and then I shook it. She had been in the bathroom for more than an hour! The bathrobe I was wearing, plus the rum, had made me warmer than usual, and a light film of perspiration formed on my forehead. I didn't want to rush the girl; I knew that Beryl was every bit as nervous as I was—but an hour and a half—Jesus!

I rapped gently on the door. "Are you all right, Beryl?"

"In a minute!" she said angrily, so savagely I started.

I backed away, and sat down on the edge of the bed, wondering what was the matter with her, why she had sounded so irritated. After an hour and a half, my question was natural enough—

The door banged open, and out she came. She was nude, defenseless, and bawling. A filmy, black nightgown was draped over her arm. She waved her right hand at me. My sweating stopped with a jar. She tried to talk, but only spluttered, and her face was distorted pitiably with her tears.

"What's the matter?" I asked, bewildered. And I felt like some kind of a monster, believing that she was crying out of fear of me.

She wiped her streaming face on the nightgown, and then threw the gadget on the floor. She breathed deeply, sighed, and gained some control over herself. "That damned thing!" she said bitterly. "I've been trying to put it in for over an hour—and I simply can't doooooo it!" A freshet of new tears began to flow, accompanied by unintelligible noises.

I put an arm around her heaving shoulders and led her to the bed. She sat down, wiping her eyes childishly with the back of her hand, and I picked up the small contrivance from the floor.

"What's the matter with it?" I asked.

"I don't know. And I paid ten dollars for it, too!"

"Well…" I hesitated. "I don't suppose—do you think I—that we could—" I tried to think of some statistical explanation that would show that conception among the sixty percent of the married couples who indulged in pre-marital intercourse was less than—

"Twelve percent," Beryl said, her eyes were streaming, "I read that too." That *too*, meant that she could read my mind. I remembered something else. Beryl had told me that she was virginal and I knew.

"I read, somewhere—that girls who—who are—"

"Virgins?" Beryl said. I stared at her.

"Yes—a doctor is supposed to do something. Did your doctor?" Beryl turned her wet face away from me. I didn't see the end of our romance yet. I knew that I would be a free man again if I moved one way…I would be committed right down the aisle with rice and shoes if the other way held a trap in the path. It was hard to think while looking at her…

"Your serve—" she said gravely. She raised her hands high, clasping each knee with her hand, and closed her eyes tightly. She turned her flushed, angry face to one side, and there was a tight quivering line in each cheek as she clenched her teeth together.

"I'll have to get dressed," I said, "and find a drugstore somewhere. Like a fool, when you said you were getting the gadget, I didn't bring anything."

"If you think I'm going to stay like this until you run all over town and come back, you've got another think coming!" she said grimly, through her clenched teeth. "My nerve won't hold out much longer. You leave me now, and when you get back I won't be here!"

There was nothing else I could do. She was brave, as strong-minded and as practical as a Dutch peasant girl, and she had suffered about as much humiliation for one day as she could stand. And I didn't blame her.

It was that simple, and that basic; and, from time immemorial it has been the only way to break the barrier that prevents a man and a woman from becoming one. But at the same moment, and I sensed it at the time, the biological trap was sprung; and poor little Buddy was conceived at the same instant.

Which meant that we were soon married, despite the careful plans we had made in our young innocence. And all because Beryl's stupid doctor had failed to mention that you can't simply buy a diaphragm at a drugstore; they have to be fitted by a physician, and the hymen, when there is one, must be slit surgically before the fitting can take place! But these were the things young couples don't learn until it's too late—no wonder gynecologists and obstetricians are rich....

To be done with it, I finished the gushy home article first when I got to the office. I wrote the cutlines for six pics, cribbing descriptions from *House Beautiful*, and turned the completed copy over to Mrs. Mosby, asking her to add a few feminine touches. So much for my turn as Mrs. Frances Worthington.

Over the telephone I got a story about a child bitten by a pet raccoon, an excited version about a drunk throwing a bowl of chile through the window of Charlie's Chile Bowl, and a poignant tale about an old boy of eighty exposing himself to some elderly ladies at the shuffleboard courts.

I had one visitor, a cute little trick in short shorts and a tight halter. She was highly excited, and she stammered. "What is it, honey?" I asked her. "Take your time."

"I just got engaged," she said, "and I want you to put it in the paper!"

"Sure, I'll put it in," I said. "Just have your daddy or mother bring me the information."

"Oh, but they don't know about it yet!" she wailed.

"And they aren't going to find out about it by reading it in the paper, either. Now, get on home and tell your folks all about your new engagement."

Bob Leanard called me and thanked me for the nice review. I was noncommittal but polite. He didn't mention Beryl's part in the play and neither did I, so the conversation was quite short.

I ate dinner at Charlie's Chile Bowl. I also pressed Charlie for details about the drunk's ire, and listened sympathetically, figuring that if I acted interested enough he would tear up my check. He did. And there was no reason for me to tell him that I had already written the story and turned it in before I left the office.

Belching fire, and with a painful, rumbling growl inside my stomach, I worked until nine P.M. on the draft of my initial article for the suicide series.

Well caught up, I picked up my car in the lot where Beryl had parked it, and drove to the high school to have a talk with Mr. Paul Hershey, Creative Writing mentor. I wondered what "Creative Writing" was supposed to be, but decided, logically, that it would be better not to really know.

Chapter Eleven

Room 103. First Floor. Lake Springs High. I paused for a moment outside the door, soaking up the reminiscent emptiness of the night-quiet corridor. A million years had passed since I had raced through these halls from one class to another. I had always been in a hurry—too many activities, too many girls, too many ideas—but I had always made it on time to the next class. And I had always made or found the time to squeeze in another club membership, attend another committee meeting, and in my senior year, to write nine-tenths of the weekly school newspaper.

Exciting days. Useless. Meaningless. Dead. I got a drink at the water fountain across the hall from Room 103. There was no monitor sitting next to the fountain to ask me for my hall pass. In the night Adult Education program, I supposed that the mature students could leave their room for a drink of water or a trip to the can without permission. I was amused by the thought of a middleaged real estate broker, for instance, taking an evening course in Business Law—and learning, to his astonishment, that for the first four weeks he was a hall monitor. In my mind I pictured him in a metal chair beside the drinking fountain....

"Excuse me, sir," he said apologetically, *"but do you have a hall pass from your teacher?"*

"Why, no!"

"Well, I don't mean anything personal, but..." He blushed, and continued embarrassedly, *"I—I—I'm the hall monitor, and*

*they told me that if a student didn't have a hall pass he wasn't
allowed to have a drink of water."*

"That's a hard rule. You know, a man being thirsty, he just —"

*"Yes, I think it is too. But what am I supposed to do? I signed
up for Business Law, and the course cost me eight-fifty. I didn't
ask to be a hall monitor."*

"Sure, sure. I guess I can wait, even if I'm not a student."

"You're not a student?"

"No, I'm a reporter, and I'm here to interview Mr. Hershey."

*"Gosh!" The paunchy broker's red face beamed as he searched
frantically through his mimeographed list of rules. "You're
okay! Go ahead and have a drink. There isn't anything in here
about restricting visitors."*

...Too bad. No monitor. Just an empty hallway, and a light
shining through the dusty transom of Room 103. Old Mrs.
Dietzmann—she of the red-red wig—had given me a C in
American History in that room, and as I remembered, it was a
better grade than I had deserved.

A woman was talking as I entered, directing her remarks to
the instructor behind the desk, but speaking loudly enough for
the others to hear her too well. I sidled along the wall and sat
down at a desk in the last row. There was another half-hour to
go, but I could stick with them for that long, I thought. The old
girl droned away, giving the class her opinion of the plot of a
short-short story that had been read aloud. She couldn't exactly
isolate it, she kept repeating, and she couldn't quite put her
finger on it, but there was something that struck her as unconvincing in the motivation, at least to her, etc.

I shut her voice away, silently counting the members of the
class. Twelve. The youngest was a male of twenty-two or -three
with shaggy black hair, and the oldest was a grandma in her
sixties, if not more. There were more women than men, and I

guessed the average age of the class to be closer to forty than to thirty. The instructor, Mr. Hershey, was surprisingly old. A tall, stooped, skeleton of a man, with deep folds of wrinkles in his neck, and a thick shock of graphite-colored hair. The collar of his white shirt was much too large, and he wore a black string tie with a cream-colored Palm Beach suit. As he listened to the woman talking, he reminded me of an old cowboy, deep in thought, trying to remember the name of the first horse he had ever ridden. When the student sat down he cleared his throat.

"Did you want to enroll?" He looked at me. "If so, you can fill in a card after class."

"No, sir," I said quickly, "but I would like to talk to you after class, Mr. Hershey."

He nodded curtly, and then addressed his remarks to the shaggy-haired young man in the first row. "You can take Mrs. Schoell's remarks for what they are worth to you, Mr. Hass, but I also have a comment of my own to make. In your story you have three named characters: Smith...Jones...Green. These are common names, granted, but I suggest, Mr. Hass, that you spend some time with a telephone book, and some better names than these ordinary ones can be found."

"I can't use the names of real people, can I?" Hass said, as he scrambled to his feet. "Why they could sue me!"

"Names picked at random from a phone book would hardly resemble your characters," Mr. Hershey said patiently. "But if you're worried about being sued, you can also change the first names. The first names in your story, John, Tom and Mary, are not very imaginative either, particularly when combined with Smith, Jones and Green."

"But Mary Green is a symbolic name!" Hass protested. "She's only *seventeen*, and already married! Don't any of you people recognize symbolism when you see it?" He whipped his fingers through his hair, and I eased myself out of the room via the back door as unobtrusively as I could.

Creative Writing. Jesus. For the remainder of the period I waited outside in the hall by the drinking fountain, smoking cigarettes, and feeling guilty about smoking on the school grounds. But there wasn't any hall monitor to catch me at it. The bell rang, and I counted the students out the door to make certain they were all gone before I re-entered. Mr. Hershey was cramming his beat-up brief case with manuscripts at the desk.

"Hudson," I said, holding out a hand, "from the *Morning News*. And Mrs. Mosby at the office, by the way, asked me to say hello for her."

"Oh, yes, I remember Mrs. Mosby well. You said you did *not* want to enroll in the class, Mr. Hudson?"

"No, sir. I want to talk about one of your former students; Mrs. Huneker."

"That name is familiar and it isn't familiar. And I've never had so many students that I—"

"She's the woman who killed herself and her two children last Monday evening."

"Of course. I read about it in the paper. For just a moment there I didn't connect the two names. She was enrolled as Marion Casselli, you see, but she hasn't been to class in three or four weeks."

"Casselli was her maiden name."

"Yes, it was in the paper. A nice girl, I thought. I had her pegged as a divorcee, but I was wrong. She was married and had two children?"

"Yes, sir. And now she's dead."

"That's right. Now she's dead."

"You don't seem to be too concerned about the tragedy, Mr. Hershey."

"My arrangement with the school is this: so long as I have ten or more students I keep my class. When I drop below ten I have to either build it up or lose it. And I have fifteen students signed for the semester. Mrs. Huneker is paid up, and I can still count her as present." He smiled then, exposing blue-gray false dentures. "I'm just talking nonsense, Mr. Hudson. Of course I'm concerned about Miss Casselli's death, but at seventy-six a man isn't easily shocked."

"Can you tell me anything about her? Why she took this course, what kind of a person she was?"

"Why should I?"

"I'm writing some follow-up articles about her case. I should've told you why in the first place."

"Right now, I've got to catch my bus home."

"I'll drive you home, Mr. Hershey."

"Are you a careful driver?" he asked anxiously.

"Yes, sir."

"All right, then, but if you drive too fast I'll have to get out of the car."

"Not over twenty-five," I promised.

After we got into the car he gave me an address in the exclusive Sea Pines residential district. I raised my eyebrows. "Teaching creative writing must pay very well," I commented.

"No need for sarcasm, Mr. Hudson. I'm paid five dollars a night, two evenings a week. The owners rent me the gate-keeper's cottage for a token rent, in order to have someone on the premises all year 'round. They're away all the summer, and even during the Season they spend most of their time at Hobe Sound and Palm Beach."

"I didn't intend to sound sarcastic," I said. "What kind of stories did Mrs. Huneker write? I'm curious."

"So far as I know she only wrote one."

"What was it about?"

"I'm not certain, or at least I'm not positive."

"You don't happen to still have a copy of it do you?"

"Yes, I have the original."

"Would you mind if I read it?"

"Yes, under the circumstances, I would mind."

"I'm not a morbid curiosity seeker, Mr. Hershey. The story Mrs. Huneker wrote wouldn't be published in the paper, not even any quotes from it. All I want to do is to find some kind of clue as to why she killed herself and two children. And if she wrote anything that might throw a little light on the subject, it would help to give me a lead to further investigations."

"I'll have to think about it."

For the rest of the way we rode in silence. I wanted him to think about it so I kept my mouth shut.

Mr. Hershey's small one-room fieldstone cottage was set well back from the gate, and surrounded by stands of coconut and monkey palms in their first or second year of growth. A large poinciana tree beside the patio in front of the house would provide ample shade in the daytime, I noted, and the patio was bordered by thickly planted multi-colored croton. A person in a hurry, driving through the gate toward the big house two hundred yards up the yellow gravel road, would probably pass the cottage without noticing it.

"I suppose you do a lot of your writing out on the patio," I said, as I followed the old man into his house.

"No, but I sit out there a lot. Sometimes I have a little wine on hand, Mr. Hudson, but not tonight. But if you'd like some instant coffee—?"

"That'll be fine. If you had mentioned it we could've picked up a bottle on the way over."

"I'm not much of a drinker." Mr. Hershey filled a boiler pan with water from the tap, and I sat down in a deep leather chair.

I was a little surprised by the Spartan simplicity of the room. There was a couch, which doubled as a bed, set below the row of back windows, and covered with a yellow spread, a pine table, and two ladder-backed maple chairs. There was a red-enamel, apartment-sized refrigerator, a white, two-burner electric stove next to the sink, and that was just about it. There were no pictures on the walls, and there were no rugs on the gleaming terrazzo floor. A pile of old magazines stacked neatly in one corner, near the foot of his couch-bed, and a portable typewriter on the table, were the only personal touches. Another door in the wall probably led to a dressing room–bathroom, and I imagined that his clothes were arranged on the racks like a soldier's for Saturday morning inspection.

Mr. Hershey brought two unmatching cups and saucers to the table, put them down, and generously spooned powdered coffee into them. I moved over to the table, and sat in one of the ladder-backed chairs across from him.

"How long have you been writing, Mr. Hershey?" There was an inadvertent patronizing note in my voice, and the old man picked it up quickly. He looked at me sharply, and then smiled, his blue-gray choppers gleaming beneath the naked bulb above the table.

"Thirty-seven years. You've never heard my name, and that worries you, doesn't it?"

"No, sir. A lot of people write on the side. I do a little writing myself."

"Well, I don't write on the side, Mr. Hudson. I've earned my living, such as it is—" he smiled sardonically, and made a sweeping motion with a long thin arm to point up the simplicity of the room "—for thirty-seven years as a full-time writer."

I whistled softly. "That isn't easy to do in America. I'd like to read some of your books, Mr. Hershey."

"I've never written a book. Only stories. And the highest

sum I ever got for a story was six hundred and fifty dollars. That was back in 1940 from the *American Legion* magazine. You see, Hudson, I've got the craftsmanship, but not the talent for big-money writing."

"If you can earn a living freelancing, I'd say you had plenty of talent, Mr. Hershey."

"No, there's a difference, and it took me a good many years to accept this difference as a fact. I have a facility, a knack, and I learned craftsmanship by writing for the pulps; westerns at a half-cent and a penny a word. That kind of writing takes facility, and a subconscious knowledge of formulas. I like to think, now, that I made the Depression a little easier to get through by giving fans a few dreams—and we did, all of us, in those days. Readers wrote long letters to the editors. They identified themselves with these tough hombres with the two, low-slung forty-fives. There was never any Depression in a western story. If a hero needed money he held up a stagecoach, or he shot a desperado for a five-hundred dollar reward. All the books ran personal columns, and the editors answered the fan letters in print." Mr. Hershey smiled, and shook his head slowly from side to side. "'Dear Waddy,' the editors all wrote."

"Today it's just about the same," I said. "We have television westerns."

"Yes, and no pulps. But it isn't the same, nothing like it used to be. During the depression, the readers wanted to be western *heroes*. Today, the kids and adults alike; they want to be western *actors* with their own TV series!"

I laughed appreciatively. "I suppose you're right. I used to read the western pulps, but I don't remember your name though."

"I used pen names, mostly. Clint Ridgeway and Red Butler were my favorites. Depended on the story I wrote. If a story didn't turn out well enough to be a Clint Ridgeway yarn, and yet it was still salable, I'd make up a new name for it, and send it to my agent. Today, though, I write under my own name...

"That water's hot now, boy. You pour it in the cups. I can lift a pot of cold water easily, but as soon as the same pot of water gets hot I have trouble with it. I get a little nervous and my hand shakes."

"You've written too many potboilers, Mr. Hershey," I said, smiling, as I crossed to the stove. I clicked off the burner and poured the water into the waiting cups.

"That's all I write today, all right," Mr. Hershey continued, "and I work pretty hard at it besides. But I've still got the knack, the touch. Every day, Monday through Friday, I write a story, and each story is exactly twelve hundred words. On Saturday morning I reread them. Two are usually impossibles and I discard them. Then I go into town and mail the other three to my agent in New York. Out of the three he usually sells at least one. Sometimes two, and sometimes none of them. They sell to a news syndicate for fifty dollars apiece. After he keeps ten percent, I get the rest, and at the end of the year I average about forty dollars a week. So that's why—in case you're interested—I teach creative writing. That ten bucks a week is for certain, and I keep it in a separate fund for stamps, type-writer ribbons and supplies."

"At least you're your own boss—say, why don't you try Mr. Curtis with some of your rejects? He's our M.E. and he used to be on the New York *Sun*. Maybe he—"

"The town's too small, son. In New York City, where the daily papers have circulation in the millions, they can run a fiction short-short once in awhile and still hit a reader percentage. For my kind of stories, the percentage of the readers, in a small town like this, wouldn't be big enough to interest your Mr. Curtis.

My newspaper shorts are good only in the big metropolitan dailies—New York, L.A., Toronto, Chicago."

"Has the paper ever done a feature on you, Mr. Hershey? I think our readers would definitely be interested in some of the things you've been telling me. I could come out here with a photographer, and—"

"No, I don't care for publicity. Not only would it not help me in any way, I'd be bothered by a gaggle of would-be writers bringing me their junk to read, or trying to get me to collaborate with them."

"A new story every day," I said admiringly. "That's really something. I don't see how you do it."

"Remember, boy, only one out of five sells. And yet, they're all the same type of story. Five times I strike the flint," he tapped the portable typewriter case with a long bony fore-finger, "and I get only one spark of fire."

"Can you give me an example?"

"If you don't mind listening. I like to be alone, but I'm alone too much, maybe, and I sort of like talking to you, Mr. Hudson."

"Richard."

"They ever call you Dick?"

I shook my head. "Not since the Eisenhower administration."

"You must be a little sensitive."

"Not really, sir. Tell me a story." I grinned.

"For a sensitive young man, you take well to torture. But all right. I wrote a story this morning, and if I don't miss my guess, it'll be the one to sell this week. A man and his wife are sitting in their kitchen, arguing about what kind of a present to get for their son's impending fourteenth birthday. The mother wants to buy him a good wristwatch, but the father's against it. He's bought the boy three different wristwatches already, cheap ones, but every time the boy has either lost the watch, or broken it, gone in swimming with it on, and so forth. So the father is adamant, saying that until the boy learns how to take care of an expensive gift like a wristwatch, he doesn't intend to buy him another.

"The boy, who has been delivering newspapers on his route, comes into the house right in the midst of the discussion. Proudly, the son rolls his sleeve back and shows off a new wristwatch to his parents. Unknown to them, he had been saving a dollar a week from his paper route to buy his own watch.

"The father is proud of the boy, knowing his son has grown old enough, at last, to accept responsibility. But the mother is saddened by the very same knowledge; she didn't want her son to be burdened with responsibilities so soon. As she prepares dinner, after the father and son go into the living room, she makes a little prayer that the boy will either break or lose his new watch before his birthday so that she can buy him one to replace it."

"You got all of that into twelve hundred words?"

"Twelve hundred and ten, to be exact."

"What's the title?"

"*No Time For Mother*. It's not much of a title, but newspaper editors usually change them anyway." He shrugged indifferently, and noisily finished his coffee.

"I like the story, Mr. Hershey," I said truthfully. "And it seems a shame to sell a story that good for only fifty dollars."

"That's all it's worth, Richard. Now any one of those female writers with three names who write for the slicks could take the same little plot and write a story that would move the readers emotionally. But I am merely a competent writer; I can't get emotion into my work. Any mother or father who reads my tale will understand it intellectually, but they won't have their emotions involved. And that's the difference between a newspaper syndicate story and a story in the *Saturday Evening Post*. And the difference between fifty dollars and a thousand arouses *my* emotions, but I can't get that into my stories either."

"Instead of writing a story every day, why don't you work all week on just one story? Maybe the extra time will help you."

"I've tried it, and do you know what happens? You refine and rewrite, and you end up without any feeling whatsoever. What it all boils down to, Richard, is this: I'm unwilling to share my real feelings with some anonymous reader. And there are very few writers who've got that kind of guts. If they did, they'd be rich and famous."

"You've given me something to think about, Mr. Hershey. But it's getting late. If you'll let me take Mrs. Huneker's story with me, I'd better get going."

"By rights, her story should be turned over to her husband. But I'm unwilling to do this because I don't think he should see it. Can you promise me that?"

"Yes, sir. Although I—"

"You'll see why after you read it. I usually type a page or so of commentary on student stories before I return them, but I never got around to critiquing this one. I didn't know exactly what to say, for one thing. And for another, it isn't really a story —I don't know what it is. Sometimes these people who decide to write, and sign up for a course, are really looking for a sort of self-therapy without knowing it. I wasn't going to read this story in class, though. At least, I wasn't planning on it without having a little talk with Marion first."

He unzipped his briefcase and searched through a dozen or so manuscripts before he found Mrs. Huneker's. It was enclosed in a manila envelope. As I got to my feet he handed it to me.

I cleared my throat. "Would you mind very much, Mr. Hershey, if I dropped around some evening and showed you the play I've been working on?"

He let his breath out audibly. "You, too?" he said sorrowfully.

I laughed. "Never mind. I'll see that you get this manuscript back, Mr. Hershey." I tapped the envelope with my palm.

"I don't want it back, Richard. When you get through with it, just tear it up and drop it into your wastebasket." He walked out to the car with me. As I started to open the door, he clasped me lightly by the shoulder. "I'll be glad to have you come around any evening, Richard. And bring your play if you like. The winter season'll be on us soon, and perhaps we can split a bottle of that wonderful California tokay. A little wine warms old bones when it's cold."

I didn't return to the office. Instead, I pointed the Chevy for the Sealbach Hotel.

For some reason, talking to Mr. Hershey had reminded me of Mr. Adamski, the old man who had wanted a "write-up" about a nonexistent anniversary. Both of these old men were the same age, seventy-six. Of the two, Adamski was far better off financially, having worked steadily for most of his life for a giant corporation. With his company pension, savings, social security, and his own home, Adamski was now able to settle down and enjoy his so-called golden years—without a worry in the world.

But not the old writer. He still struggled along every day, barely getting by, following the hopeless American Dream, still trying, and still not making it. And I supposed that Mr. Hershey was reconciled by now to the almost certain knowledge that he would never make it. Why, then, did I feel only pity for Old Man Adamski, when I felt a respectful admiration for Old Man Hershey? To be fair, it had taken an equal amount of determination for Adamski to stick it out for forty years in a dead-end job as it had for Hershey to come up with a new idea for a short-short story every morning.

Ahh, Hudson, I thought disgustedly, you think too much; and you have a long way to go before you sleep.

Chapter Twelve

Every person who lives in a city, even a small city like Lake Springs, needs at least one secret place where they can go at any time and truly be alone. In the office there were people and a phone that rang; at home there was a wife and a child. But I had found my little secluded spot where I could stay for as long as I liked and know, with confidence, that I wouldn't be interrupted or disturbed. Astrology is supposedly a false science, but I was a Capricorn, and astrologists say that men born during the Month of the Goat have an affinity for cabalas, conundrums and clandestine hiding places.

Dave Finney, who was also a Capricorn, told me once that when he wanted to get away from people he drove down the highway to the Bird Farm eighteen miles from Lake Springs, and talked to the parrots and macaws for a couple of hours. These wise birds had the right answers for everything, he said. To a question such as, "What is life really all about?" his favorite bird, a blue-and-yellow macaw would reply: "Hello, Kiddo," "Toast and coffee," or "You're a sweet bird, you are," and then go into paroxysms of laughter. Dave maintained that these were all valid answers to the perplexities of life; and perhaps he was right.

My hiding place was the seldom-used Men's Lounge on the mezzanine floor of the Sealbach Hotel. By entering the hotel via the parking lot side door and climbing a short flight of stairs, not even the man on the desk knew that I was ensconced in the lounge. There was a lobby lavatory that guests used, and another small men's room beside the cocktail lounge, so the mezzanine lounge was rarely entered. The room was air-conditioned, and furnished with two deep leather chairs, a cigarette table, a floor lamp, and a threadbare, rose-colored carpet.

This was the perfect place, in my opinion, to read Marion Huneker's short story. I lit a cigarette, opened the envelope, and pulled out a dozen typed sheets of light-gray monogrammed stationery. I remembered the stationery from my brief glimpse of her suicide note. I shivered slightly, as I started to read the story, but that was caused by the air-conditioned coolness of the lounge…

LITTLE MRS. LITTLE

By Marion Casselli

With a tiny gasp of fright little Mrs. Little turned over in bed and put her small hand to her mouth. Oh, but that had been such a bad dream! She wondered if she had cried out in her sleep. She guessed not. He still snored away beside her, a noisy, pink elephant covered with the blue electric blanket, although His half of the blanket wasn't turned on. Mrs. Little felt in the dark for the switch to turn her side of the blanket down.

My, but she was warm! All of that walking and walking in her dream had made her perspire freely. She had been lost for two days, wandering in a strange city, and she had been frightened. She had wondered if her Husband would worry about her, but she knew that He didn't care, or He wouldn't be so mean about the checkbook.

Little Mrs. Little got out of bed, wrapping her quilted pink doll's robe about her shoulders, and slipped her tiny little feet into pink slippers, all toasty warm with silky rabbit fur. Like always, when she awakened in the night, she had to go to the bathroom for a minute. In the bathroom, afterwards, she was drawn to the study of her heart-shaped face in the mirror. She looked at her rosy tongue, and fluffy pink hair, touching it up with the tips of her fingers.

There was a faint network of tiny furrows on each of her temples, and one long deep frown line sliding across the middle of her otherwise smooth forehead. She frowned and the line deepened. Then she stamped one tiny foot on the tiled floor. "Oh, but I mustn't frown, she said aloud to her face in the mirror, I mustn't!" She smiled at her image in the mirror, nodding fatuously, and was immediately overwhelmed with an attack of the giggles. She clapped both hands over her mouth as her Husband groaned in bed and turned over. The tortured springs groaned back in protest at His movement.

"It's all His fault that I can't sleep," she thought petulantly. "He insists that I balance my checkbook myself, and He knows perfectly well that I can't do it!" But the hour was late and Mrs. Little was more tired than she realized and she couldn't sustain her anger at her Husband at this ungodly hour in the early morning. She drank a little water, gargled with mouthwash to make her mouth taste better, and then went back to bed and to sleep. This time without any dreams.

The next morning over coffee, long after her Husband had gone to His office, little Mrs. Little hopelessly went over her accounts again. Somewhere, even though she had gone through both bank statements several times with the point of her tiny gold pencil, there were several checks that simply must be missing. She was proud of one important error she had caught, and all by herself too! She had numbered three of the cancelled checks all the same: #63. And that might be where the error lay. The lost checks still unaccounted for might also be numbered 64, or even 63 again. She had absolutely no head for numbers and her Husband knew it. In five minutes He could have had the account all in order but He had said, No!

"And until you get it balanced," He had said, "I forbid you to write another single check!"

It wasn't as though we were poor, Mrs. Little fumed helplessly. There is all kinds of money in the bank and He is making more and more every day! She felt like crying but she didn't because once she let go she would go on and on and she would have to wash her face afterwards and then her coffee would be cold.

She straightened the stack of odd-sized bills and arranged the two leather bankbooks on either side to look like little wings. The big pile of cancelled checks looked simply terrible, and she covered the pile with the two legal-looking yellow bank statements. She was neat! Her Husband couldn't deny her that much! But now she did not know which way or to who else to turn to.

On Monday she had asked her mother but her mother couldn't help her. "You know, dear, how I am with figures!"

And then on Tuesday she had gone to see her best friend, Laura Lou. After Laura Lou had looked at everything she had given up completely without even trying. "This is a mess, darlin', a real mess!"

She hadn't needed Laura Lou to tell her that! She knew it was a mess. She had needed help and Laura Lou had offered her a martini and a good one, but not accounting experience.

Little Mrs. Little's last hope had been Miss Tuttle, a girl she had known in school and who taught school herself now. She had had Roger, her chauffeur, drive her over to Miss Tuttle's house. (She lived in a project housing area of all places). Roger had been embarrassed. There had been all those children around, and Roger had had a time keeping them away from the car.

And then over tea and delicious pecan Brownies little Mrs. Little had completely forgotten all about the purpose of her visit until it was time to leave. There had been so many good things to talk about and she had loved Sally Tuttle so in school. And she felt foolish to ask Sally to take a look at her checkbooks for her. It would look like she had spent her money foolishly, and indeed there had been some foolish expenditures, and why not? God knows He had the money. So they had kissed each other good-by and Mrs. Little had cried a little on the way home in the car. Only stopping at the good French ice cream place and sending Roger in for a double dip chocolate chip cone had stopped her tears.

And now little Mrs. Little became aware of the doorbell which had been ringing persistently for some time now without being noticed or answered. "Oh, answer it," she thought and then she remembered that the cook was shopping.

Little Mrs. Little floated through the rooms to the door, her long pink negligee trailing her, dragging along the carpet like a train. Size seven was too large and what she really needed was a six and a quarter.

"Come in!" Mrs. Little said cordially to the man in the doorway. He looked like a gentleman and he talked like a gentleman only very fast. As he talked to her so fast she listened half with her eyes and half with her checkbook. Hardly any with her mind because she had made up her mind almost from the time he had opened his mouth.

"And so you see, Mrs. Little," the insurance salesman concluded, with a practiced smile, "this extra coverage is really mandatory, if you look at it practically, and I don't see how you can do otherwise."

Little Mrs. Little closed her eyes and smiled. "My Husband has a fifty-thousand dollar policy already, but your plan sounds terribly attractive."

"And so economical." Her tiny pink hand stopped him from going on.

"I'll take it on one condition." She opened her eyes and batted her long pink lashes. "Balance my checkbook for me!"

"Why that's easy!" the salesman replied. "Why the homemakers I call on often ask me to balance their checkbooks for them!"

Five minutes later the salesman chuckled. "And there you are, Mrs. Little! To the penny! If I may make a suggestion, I'd get only one checking account instead of two, and you'll find it easier to keep in order."

"Thank you. Write the new policy and come by tomorrow morning and I'll give you a check for the full amount."

When the salesman left, little Mrs. Little sighed happily and made a fresh pot of coffee. The new policy would ensure her house, paid in full, upon His death. There remained now the single problem of killing Him and getting the full $50,000 in cash! Oh, but that would be hard! Getting rid of her healthy Husband would be a task! But little Mrs. Little would be able to find a way. She was sure that she oould!

She had balanced her checkbook, hadn't she?

The End

Chapter Thirteen

Before attempting to evaluate Mrs. Huneker's meretricious story I read it three times. On the back of the brown envelope I jotted down my impressions and then tried to objectively sum them up:

1. There was a plot, of sorts, but the motivation was much too weak for the projected murder of the protagonist's husband.

2. The capitalization of "He" and "Husband" throughout the script may or may not have been an attempt to establish the husband either as a deity or a father-figure against whom, the *little* wife, was powerless.

3. Not once, until the contrived, coincidental arrival of the insurance salesman—who came to *her*—had Mrs. Little turned to a male to help her solve her dilemma. In each case she had asked assistance from another woman, and each female was as ineffectual as the heroine.

4. There was a feeble attempt at humor in the story, but it was about as funny as a crutch. Had she meant it to be as funny as a crutch, and was that a disguised symbol?

5. Because the insurance salesman had straightened out the checkbooks in five minutes—the same time she had established earlier that her own husband could have done it—had she meant to imply that all men were alike?

6. Did the bills, bank statements and checkbooks add up to a woman trying to set up some "checks and balances" in her own life? And was that woman Marion Huneker?

7. There was no foreshadowing on the abrupt decision to kill her husband. It read more as an afterthought; as a way to resolve the story in a hurry.

8. I found no misspelled words. This couldn't possibly have been her first short story. Surely, in school, or prior to her enrollment in Hershey's class, she had written stories before.

About then, at my eighth note, I gave up my analysis as a bad job. If the story about little Mrs. Little was an allegory, there was no point in trying to puzzle out the meanings, and besides, I had a hunch that it was merely an attempt at a mystery story, and not a very good try at that. I didn't really know the deceased woman well enough to make a valid judgment on the story. I was trying too hard, and in all probability, attributing powers, subtlety and insight to a woman who had merely tried her hand at a short-short story. The manner in which she had killed her children had been as subtle as a hurricane.

The only clue worth noting, and it wasn't worth much, was the fact that she had tried to write a mystery-type story, or at least a half-hearted mystery. Why had she chosen that form instead of another; instead of a love story, for instance? Was life itself a mystery to the woman, or had she written the story in mystery form because they were supposed to be the easiest kind to write?

Sitting in that quiet lounge, my nostrils filled with the sweet smell of the pink cake of deodorizing soap in the urinal, my evaluations all added up to one fat zero.

I returned the story to the envelope. A few of her phrases, taken out of context, would add spice to my article about her death, at least, so the story wasn't a total loss. There was one effect the story had on me that rankled. Never again would I be able to retreat to this hidden lounge for a relaxing hour without thinking about Mrs. Huneker. I would have to find another hiding place...

When I got back to the office I hid the manuscript in the bottom right-hand drawer of my desk. There was nothing pressing to do, so I typed a few comments about Paul Hershey, and made some notes for the future questioning of the old mentor. He was feature story material, whether he wanted publicity or not, and at some future date I was going to call on him again and bring a photographer with me. No man who had devoted thirty-seven years of his life to getting his name into print could have a valid objection about seeing it in print again.

I got home at twelve-thirty and Beryl was still up, frying bacon in the kitchen. We had a reconciliation of sorts. I put my arms around her waist and kissed the nape of her neck. She pulled away from me, not in anger, but because she was busy.

"Ahhh!" I said. "You smell like you've just had a bath, and such sweetness, combined with the fragrance of frying bacon, is enough to drive a man mad!"

"Look out!" She jabbed a sharp elbow into my stomach. "I'm busy."

"Are you, by any chance, making a bacon-and-tomato sandwich?"

"I am."

"If I were to put two more pieces of bread into the toaster; would you make me one too?"

"I guess I'll have to," she sighed, "or I won't enjoy mine. Get the bacon out of the fridge and put the mayonnaise on the table."

"How did the play go tonight?" I asked, as I helped prepare the sandwiches.

"There was a bit of a cast let down tonight, but we've got a full house for tomorrow night, and everybody's all excited about it. I goofed my lines three times tonight, and I felt bad about it because Buddy was watching the play."

"How did Buddy like it?"

"He complained about the direction."

"Direction? What does an eight-year-old boy know about direction?"

"Our boy has been brought up on television, and don't forget it. He said, and this is what he said exactly, 'There was too much moving around by that man with the cigar. I kept watching him to see what he'd do and then I didn't hear what you said sometimes.'"

"Movement without motivation." I laughed delightedly. "He was referring to Fiscur, of course. That's a damned shrewd observation for a boy to make, and the next time I see Bob Leanard I'm going to tell him about it."

"I thought it was, too. And now, of course, Buddy wants to get into a play!"

"It wouldn't hurt him any. If they do anything with children this season, maybe we can ease him in to something." While we ate the wonderful bacon-and-tomato sandwiches and drank tall glasses of milk, we discussed Buddy and, for a change, our conversation was quite pleasant. Beryl was a good mother, as well as being a good wife. And working six nights a week, I certainly didn't give her any help with the boy. I felt a trifle guilty—

"Beryl," I blurted impulsively, "I'm sorry about that stupid review. You were really very good as Julie, but to tell you the truth, the real reason I didn't give you the review you deserved was on account of the people at the Civic Theater. You know what a bunch of backbiters they all are, and if I'd built you up the way you should have been, they'd have said it was because you're my wife. This way, you see, you'll get a lot of sympathy from the theater members, and I'll be the villain. Believe me, it's better this way."

"I love you, Richard," she said, swallowing a big bite at the same time. "I only took the part to please you—"

"And you did, honey. I was very proud of you."

"What you think is all that matters. I'm sick and tired of the whole business; the boring rehearsals and all. I'm sorry I kept the part a secret from you, too. That was real dumb."

"Next time you want to do some acting let me know." I patted her arm. "I'll write a part that'll fit you."

"I don't think there'll be a next time," she said grimly.

"Wake me at seven-thirty. Saturday, you know, and a busy day for me."

"I'm going to let Buddy sleep late. He was up till almost eleven-thirty and that's pretty late for him—"

"I didn't say anything about Buddy! He can sleep all day. I said wake *me* up at seven-thirty!"

"Don't I always wake you? Why are you snapping at me?" She said this so reasonably I almost did snap at her, wondering at my unreasonableness.

"I'm sorry," I apologized. "I'm tired, I suppose."

"I'm tired, too. Did you ever think of that?"

I was on the point of telling her that if she had stayed home where she belonged, instead of entering into secret alliances with a bunch of would-be actors, she wouldn't be so tired—but I caught myself, in time. That little business had been settled already. Why bring it up again? And why was I deliberately courting an argument? She wasn't the guilty party, I was; and knowing I was guilty, I was on the defensive. That was it. But so far, she didn't know anything about my shenanigans—thank the Lord!

I shifted uneasily; there were thousands of ties that bound us together. She deserved better—well, I would make it up to her.

"Right," I said cheerfully, although my voice sounded some-what hollow. "We're both tired, and we'd better go to bed."

Although I was in no mood for love-making, a shower revived me somewhat, and as I sat on the edge of the bed, smoking a contemplative cigarette and waiting for Beryl to join me, the pleasure of anticipation gradually aroused my desire. But even my anticipation was marred by the awareness of my guilt. What really bothered me most, however, was the mixed-up way I felt about everything. I wasn't certain whether my feeling of guilt was sincere because of slipping around on Beryl, or whether it was caused by the idea that Beryl might find out about it. But how could she find out? I'd never tell her—and *Gladys* would never tell her. And as this load lifted from my mind, I won-dered why I didn't feel any better about the situation…

Beryl came into the bedroom. She held a towel around her waist with one hand, but her full white breasts nodded to me in unison as she leaned over to open the middle drawer in the dresser for one of her nightgowns.

"I really am tired, Richard," she said, watching me snuff out the cigarette.

"All right." I smiled. "A good night kiss and a good night's sleep is all we need."

"No argument?"

"Of course not." I affected surprise. "You don't think I'd force you to do anything against your will, do you?"

She laughed. "I've heard tell…" She nodded solemnly.

"Rumors, Mrs. Hudson. Nothing but rumors."

She slipped into her ridiculous, inadequate shorty nightgown, put her hands behind her, and leaned down to kiss me. Her breasts, like two firm, rubber balls, rolled half way out of the loose fitting top, and bounced in unison—one, two, three, a-lary…

I kissed her warm, soft mouth, marvelling at the sweet, green smell of her skin and hair. "Well," I said, grinning, pulling my head away as the kiss gave indications of continuing for some time, "Good night!" I rolled over to my side of the bed, yawning audibly.

"Good night," she replied, snapping off the light.

A moment later she lay beside me, and her chin rested on my bare shoulder.

"I've heard tell," she said softly, musingly, "that some married folks, not even married as long as us, never do make love."

"I've heard the same thing. But I don't believe it. Do you?"

"Not for a minute!" In the darkness, her hand lightly touched my thigh. The muscles of my leg tautened, and her hand inched higher. I turned toward her, and she pressed herself against me, breathing quickly as I ran my hand down her back to pull her in even tighter while the other hand caressed the round hillocks that arched and quivered in response to the growing underground spasms...

"But not us, Richard? Huh? Ever?"

...around the bend of her hips where the hand lingered awhile contemplating the terrain. Then up...up...up the rising landscape until coming to an unsettled rest on one quaking mound blossoming with a single, pink flower.

"No, not us," I whispered huskily, covering her mouth with my own; and strangely moved, I repeated over and over again in my head, in rhythm with our love-making, "Never, never, never, never, never..."

On Saturdays I usually got to the office at noon, which was an early hour to go to work, but on this particular Saturday I reported in at 10:00 A.M., a ridiculously early hour. For the past couple of weeks I had been sluffing off so many little things, they had all stacked up on me. There was a formidable amount of work to be done in my wire HOLD basket. The wedding and engagement stories, which had to be written sooner or later, had built upon each other to an all-time high.

As a matter of policy, we printed, in the Sunday paper, a story about every wedding that took place during the week. The couple concerned would buy at least a dozen copies of that edition to send to friends and relatives, and why not run the wedding story in the Sunday paper which cost ten cents instead of the daily paper that only came to five?

To obtain information about engagements and weddings the paper had two mimeographed forms for the use of those concerned. When the fathers or mothers or brides-to-be made their assault upon the office to obtain "write-ups" they were handed one of these forms which precluded the overlooking of any pertinent information, e.g. "What was the Maid (Matron) of Honor wearing?" and "What were the presents given to the bridesmaids?" The forms, which Mrs. Mosby had prepared, were so complete that many parents took extra forms home, noticing that they had neglected some very important items in their wedding preparations.

To those concerned, an engagement or a wedding was news. To me, however, they were not news. If an engagement announcement or a wedding was reported a week or so late it made no difference to me. But some of the forms in my basket, with 8 x 10 photos attached, had been there for three full weeks, and they were already too late to make the next day's Sunday edition, which had been run off on Friday. So I was forced to write these wretched stories now. I was so far behind that I knew a few of the irate mothers had called the M.E. already to complain. And when he got around to jumping me I wanted to be able to tell him that they were written and turned in.

I worked sedulously for four miserable hours and reduced the pile of forms down to the current week before I knocked off for lunch. At two-thirty I returned to the office and made some routine calls to my spies here and there about town. The Monday *Morning News* was always a sketchy paper, but the news items had to be written on Saturday or I wouldn't have my Sundays free.

The County Tax Assessor was always good for an item—he loved to make statements. The Postmaster was also a good source of information. If nothing else, he could be quoted as saying that mail deposited at the Post Office after 6:00 P.M. wouldn't reach New York for two days. There were always enough tourists in town to rerun a statement of that kind. I had other fine spies as well; a cute blonde secretary in the Chamber of Commerce office who hated the manager; an embittered court reporter who was forced to take down the minutes of the City Commission meetings without being paid any extra money for the job; and every single member of the hotel and motel association. They furnished me with the names and activities of their important and unimportant guests alike. And a name printed is a paper sold.

If I had been the kind of reporter who is satisfied with secondhand information, I could have written enough copy to satisfy the M.E. every night without leaving my desk. Lake Springs was too small to support any full-time press agents, but I sometimes thought that every resident of the city spent all of his waking hours scheming of a way to get his name into the paper. If an old lady planned a weekend visit to a cousin in Orlando she would phone this earthshaking event in to the paper. And what was worse; if the item wasn't printed she would call and again and demand to know why it wasn't printed. Back during the hula-hoop craze, I had had fifteen calls one evening from idiotic mothers—each of them claiming the world endurance record in hoop-spinning for their insufferably well-coordinated brats!

By six that evening I had turned over enough copy to Harris for the Monday A.M. edition to ease my conscience. The weekly stipend, small as it was, that Mrs. Mosby handed me every Saturday, always had the effect of making me do a little more work than I did on weeknights. In this respect, I was like the majority of the reporters I had known and talked to about this extra payday effort.

All of us had a deep-seated but definite fear of being fired and blackballed—and ending up as an instructor of journalism at a junior college somewhere. This was a recurrent dream that every active reporter had to learn to live with. More than one night I had awakened from a dead slumber, perspiring, trembling and afraid, caught up in a vivid nightmare of screaming, pimply, junior college students.

To sustain myself for another three hours I sent Blake, the Negro office boy, out for a container of coffee and two hamburgers. I worked until nine on my first article for the suicide series. This was a general piece on suicide, well-larded with statistics, both real and imagined, and I thought it read fairly well. With Mrs. Mosby's help I dug through the negative morgue, looking for a photograph gruesome enough—that still wouldn't offend anybody—to illustrate the article.

There weren't any decent shots of suicides, but I had a brilliant idea. There was an excellent art shot of a little girl bawling that one of the photographers had taken at Bersen's Department Store a few years back. Actually, the little girl was crying because her mother had wanted her to sit in Santa Claus' lap. But our readers were unaware of that fact.

I cropped the 4x6 proof to show just the tearful eyes, runny nose, and anguished, open mouth, and asked Mrs. Mosby to have it blown up to a six-column cut. With a nice overline such as, WHY DID MY DADDY KILL HIMSELF?, very few readers would be able to ignore the accompanying article...

Feeling well-pleased with myself I left the office, bought a pint of cheap bourbon at a package store, and drove to Mr. Jack Huneker's residence. Either Jack Huneker held the key to his wife's death or he didn't, and the only way to find out was to pump him.

Chapter Fourteen

I parked across from the Huneker residence and opened my bottle to take a nip before crossing the street. I changed my mind about the drink once the seal was broken, however, and replaced the pint in my jacket pocket. I had purchased Old Indian, a very cheap brand, and I thought it would be judicious to offer the first drink to Jack Huneker so he could take the fusel oil off the top.

There was a view of the black lake beyond Huneker's house and, where his lawn swooped down to the beach, there was a single pole light burning above his white, private boat dock. The Venetian blinds were down over the picture window facing the street, but some light shone through, and as I approached the narrow front porch I could hear dance music and the voice of a sports announcer competing against each other.

The bicycle and toys were no longer on the porch. The front door was open, and through the aluminum screened door I looked into the living room which was lighted by a standing floor lamp and the blue television screen. For a moment, I hesitated, not seeing Huneker, and then I pushed the buzzer and waited.

Huneker answered, calling from the depths of the house: "Just a minute!"

And when he called, in a deep monotone, I had a momentary feeling of perplexing panic. I wanted to bolt and say the hell with it. My visit, I felt, was not only purposeless but an invasion of the man's personal tragedy. At last, however, Huneker came to the door, and switched on the overhead porchlight from inside, activating a flutter of slumbering moths. He was a big man with dark curling hair, and a square, blunt-featured face in need of a shave. He wore a pair of gray wash-pants, sandals without socks, and a blue silk, short-sleeved sport shirt. There was a four-inch band of black silk basted onto the short left sleeve. In my sudden confusion I still had presence of mind, and I made a mental note of this mourning band. It was ludicrous, but oddly touching, to see a mourning band on a shiny electric blue sport shirt. This point would make good copy. Thinking this, I was ashamed…

"Sorry you had to wait," Huneker said, raising a plate of sandwiches he held in his right hand. "I was in the kitchen."

"My name is Hudson." I took the pint out of my jacket. "I was in the neighborhood, and I thought I'd drop by and offer you a drink."

"That's a switch," he said mordantly, eyeing the bottle. "I've been overrun with neighbors the last couple of days bringing me food." He smoothed his hair with his free hand. "They must think I'm starving or something; me with a freezerful of steaks."

"It's an old Southern custom to bring food when there's been a death in the family, Mr. Huneker."

"I remember you now," he said, narrowing his eyes. "You're a reporter. I saw you on the night—" He turned to put the plate down on the foyer table, and I noticed he was a little unsteady on his feet. "You can get the hell out of here!"

"Sure. I don't have any business here, and I apologize. Your wife just happened to be a friend of mine, and I only dropped around to pay my respects. Good night, Mr. Huneker." As I turned away he unlatched the screen, door and pushed it open.

"Just a minute, Hudson. You don't have to get so damned huffy. At least you offered me a drink. Come in and I'll buy you one."

I followed him into the living room. An announcer talked

rapidly as he described a basketball game; his voice came from a small, red radio on top of the television set. The picture of the TV set was on, but not the sound, and cowboys galloped quietly across the scene. The music I had heard from outside issued from three strategically placed speakers, and I recognized the slow melody as one of Jackie Gleason's arrangements.

Huneker had had several, I figured, but he marched resolutely to the rattan bar in front of the imitation fireplace, and spoke over his shoulder. "What'll you have? Name it, and I've got it."

"Bourbon and water."

"Then I guess you'll settle for Jack Daniel. Black label," he added, as he lifted the bottle.

"You bet." I sat down on the divan without being asked.

"How come you just happened to drop around tonight?" Huneker frowned, as he handed me a tall one. "I don't know you, Hudson, and the story's all over with."

"I knew Marion fairly well," I lied. "We were in the writing class together, at the Adult Education Center."

"Oh!" He nodded, apparently satisfied. "That's a little different, then. Marion had a lot of friends here, more'n I knew she had. She told me she was taking some kind of night school course but I didn't know it was writing till I saw it in the paper. That's the kind of girl Marion was, always doing something different...but not for very long. That was her main trouble, boredom, and not sticking to anything long enough to like it. All this crap." He shook the ice in his half empty glass to indicate the room or the fact that his glass was half empty. "Too much for her maybe." He drained the rest, put two fresh ice cubes in the glass, and added whiskey.

"You ought to put a little water in that," I suggested.

"Yes, I suppose I should," he said reflectively, sitting down across the cocktail table from me in a deep chair. "But I like the heavy taste. It's beginning to get to me anyway, so I won't have another till you finish yours…Take all night if you want; I didn't ask you to slug it. Here," he pushed the plate of sandwiches toward me. "Take one. Ham and cheese, with plenty of hot mustard."

"No, thanks."

Huneker bit greedily into a thick sandwich, and talked with his mouth full. "I didn't eat nothin' all day. Then I figured I'd better eat something whether I was hungry or not. The neighbors brought all kinds of stuff over; a whole ham, a big pot of baked beans. There's a couple of pies and a chocolate cake in the kitchen if you don't want a sandwich."

"The only reason I stopped," I said, "was due to not seeing any cars parked out in front. If the house had been full of people, I'd've come by another time."

"There were all kinds of people here yesterday, and I didn't know half of 'em, just like I don't know you. But I kind of eased 'em all out. Thought I wanted to be alone. But I guess I'm not quite ready to be alone, after all."

Watching him closely to see what kind of reaction I would get, I said: "The choice wasn't really yours, Mr. Huneker."

"That's where you're wrong. Hudson? That's like the car, right?"

I nodded. "The same."

"Catholic?"

I shook my head. "Nothing."

"That's me." He wiped his mouth with the back of a hairy hand. "I'm not really a Catholic, Hudson. Marion refused to marry me until I took instructions, and I joined later on just to keep her mouth from flapping about it. But I never believed in it."

"You had an official Requiem Mass—"

"That was for the benefit of her soul." He smiled sardonically. "She would've wanted it that way. And it'll probably cost me a stained glass window, too." He shrugged indifferently. "But that can be deducted."

"Here," I said, putting my pint on the coffee table. "Have one on me."

Huneker picked up the bottle and shook his head sadly as he read the label. "Old Indian...Jesus! I haven't seen any of this stuff in years. But I used to drink it; I've drunk plenty of it! This stuff'll kill you in the morning, Hudson."

"I know. But you don't buy Jack Daniel's whiskey on a reporter's salary."

"You're getting by, aren't you?"

"Yes. I'm getting by."

"Then don't bitch. Married?"

"Yes, one child. A boy."

"My boy was eight. Tony."

"We call our son Buddy, but his real name is Theodore, after my wife's father. A hell of a name, Theodore."

"You could call him Ted."

"Then the other kids would call him Teddy, and I prefer Buddy."

"You're a Southerner, aren't you, Hudson?"

"This is my hometown, and I know all the words to *Dixie*."

"Tell me something," he said seriously, frowning, and leaning forward in his chair. "Why in the hell do they call so many of the boys Bubba down here? I got three different men working for me named Bubba!"

I laughed at his earnestness. "It's usually a boy from a good-sized family, especially an older boy with two or three younger sisters. Young girls have a tendency to lisp more than young boys, and they call their older brother Bubba because they can't say Brother. That's all. And the name Junior isn't popular in the South, so many Juniors are also called Bubba."

"I don't give a damn what they call each other down here. I'm only making conversation; you know that, don't you?" He shook his head, rattled the ice in his empty glass.

"Suits me. I haven't got anything else to do."

"Fine. Believe I will try some of your Old Indian, but for this stuff I will add a little water!"

"It's even better with Coca-Cola. Then you can hardly taste it."

Huneker smiled. "You're all right, Hudson. Give me your glass and I'll freshen it. With Jack Daniel's, not the Old Indian."

As Huneker replenished the glasses I realized that there was something about the man that I liked. He was more human, now, than he had been on the night of his wife's death. Talking to the detective, he had been cool and collected, he had shown no emotion whatsoever. I had attributed his assured manner to numbness at the time, but now—maybe because he had had a few drinks—he seemed like any normal guy who was a little lonely when the wife was away for a few days.

"I'd better slow down a little," he said, after a perfunctory taste of the Old Indian and water. He wet his lips, put the glass down, and shoved it away from him. "I keep trying to think about something else, anything else, but it isn't easy." He looked at me belligerently, and lifted his square prognathic chin. "If you're like everybody else around town, you've got some kind of a theory, or *real* reason why my wife killed herself—haven't you?"

"No, not really," I said easily, "except that she may have killed herself because she found out about you and Helen Devereaux."

I fully expected him to take a swing at me, after a remark like that; but I didn't mind a fight, and I was confident that I could take him without too much trouble. And beside, a good rough-and-tumble might have cheered the poor devil up considerably. His reaction was the opposite of what I expected, however. The corners of his mouth turned down, and he looked at me with puzzled bewilderment.

"That's a damned rotten thing to say, Hudson."

"You brought it up," I shrugged indifferently. "Otherwise I wouldn't have said anything."

"Well, no matter what you happen to think, *that* isn't true! I'll tell you exactly what killed Marion. Prosperity. It's like the difference between drinking good whiskey and Old Indian. Jack Daniel's and Old Indian are both whiskey, and you can get just as drunk on one as you can on the other. The difference is that when you can afford to drink Jack Daniel you can afford to drink it all the time. But when you have to drink Old Indian, it's an occasion—and you wouldn't want it around all the time."

"I may be dense, Huneker, but I don't follow that line of reasoning. If you're trying to tell me that Marion was an alcoholic, I won't buy it. I know that she wasn't."

"Maybe I can put it another way." He shook his head, and pursed his lips in thought. "I've been thinking of nothing else for two full days, Hudson. Hell, I haven't been in bed or slept morn'n an hour or so since it happened, and my head's going around and around. But now, I think I know most of the answers. Marion wasn't even close to being an alcoholic—I didn't mean that. She'd have been better off if she had taken a few too many drinks once in awhile. It helps to blow off steam sometimes, but I may be wrong there, too. But I do know this: the first three years we were married we were happy.

"We lived in a trailer, and it was a practical way to live, because I was following construction jobs all around the country. Then, after Tony was born, Marion got the idea that a trailer camp was no place to bring up a child. To please her, I eventually got enough dough together to come down here and go into business for myself. As for myself, I liked construction work better, but you're a married man and you know what a wife's pressure can do sometimes. Building roads, excavation work, that was my line; I was a heavy equipment operator, and I liked it because I felt like I was doing something worthwhile. Do you know what I mean?"

"I know exactly what you mean. So far."

"Maybe I can sort it all out. I'm not a good businessman, but I've made good money anyway. I don't have any business education to begin with, just high school, and I didn't graduate. But perhaps because I didn't respect my business, I've felt contempt for all the money I've made right from the start. The more I made, the more reckless I got with it, not giving a damn. And that made me more money again. That's the secret to my success here, and a lot of people hate my guts for it. I took bids a hell of a lot lower than I should have, but I still made money, and did a good job, too. All of a sudden I had a good reputation, and people started buying from me because they knew I didn't cheat and did a good job on my materials. After the first year and a half I couldn't handle all of the orders I was getting so I jacked up my prices to cut down the volume. But the stupid bastards were willing to pay the higher prices, so I was forced to expand. It's all a little crazy…"

"What's this got to do with Marion?"

"She had it too good, that's all! Too easy, not enough to do; and because I was busy all the time, I bought her presents and gave her a big bank account and all…" He nodded, sipped from his glass. "What I should've done was to belt her once in awhile, knock a little sense in her head."

"Do you really believe that?" I said disbelievingly.

"I know it! I'm selling out here, Hudson, lock, stock and barrel.

I'm going to buy me a flashy trailer and a good pick-up truck and hit the road; start working with my hands again."

"And what about your little girlfriend? Helen?"

"How'd you happen to find out about her, anyway?" he asked curiously, but I didn't detect any resentment in his voice.

"This is a small town; small for a man who gets around the way I do."

"Then you must know that Helen is just another bang around town—so why are you trying to make something out of it?"

"Because of the children, that's why. When your wife killed herself, that was her right and privilege. But she also killed your children, and that's a form of feminine revenge. And I'm inclined to think that she was trying to get even with you for stepping out of line. I don't know what else to think."

"Marion wasn't a mean or petty woman, Hudson. You didn't know her the way I did or you wouldn't make a stupid remark like that. She was really a sweet girl, a religious girl; a daily communicant, for Christ's sake! In her mixed-up way, and that's all it was, she truly believed that she was taking her children to a better place. She read too much; she always had her nose in a magazine or a book. She even worried about atom bombs. She came to me one day all excited about the atom tests, afraid the kids would get fallout dust in their bones from drinking milk. She said if they kept on testing those bombs our grandchildren would be born with two heads, and maybe twelve fingers. And do you know where she got all that stuff? Out of magazines."

"There's a lot of truth in it, Huneker."

"What if there is? There isn't anything you or me can do about it, is there? If some of my employees had twelve fingers, maybe I could get a decent day's work out of 'em. Life goes on, Hudson, and the world has a way of getting rid of the ones who can't take it. Sitting here today, and all last night, drinking along slow to keep a nice edge on, I figured I had two choices open. I could either stay here in Lake Springs, brooding about Marion and the kids for the rest of my life, or I could start all over again. I'm only thirty-six, a young man, and I'm starting over. Why shouldn't I? And the next time, by God, I'm not going to marry some good-looking young girl right out of a convent! What I want is a down-to-earth, hard-working widow who's been left with two or three kids, a woman who's washing clothes or something to support 'em, and laughing about it. That's the kind of a wife a man like me needs.

"And if I get sore and sock her one because dinner isn't ready or something when I get home from work, she'll sock me right back. Then we can make it all up in bed, the way a man and his wife are supposed to do. If I ever so much as raised my voice to Marion she sulked for a week. She'd go off into the bedroom and lock the door and cry. I got so I was afraid to open my mouth around here, and I couldn't put so much as a finger on the kids, no matter what they did!"

"You're whistling in the dark, Huneker."

"Maybe I am. But I'm doing something. What would you do?"

"I'll take another drink, and then I'd better go."

"Guess we'd better have another short one, at that. I had me a nice mellow edge when you got here, but now I've talked it all away."

I crossed to the bar, poured a one-ounce shot, and tossed it off. Then I brought the bottle of Jack Daniel to the coffee table, and put it down in front of Huneker. He shook his head, put the cap back on my bottle of Old Indian, and handed it to me. "No, I'd better not have another one, Hudson. The smart thing for me to do now is hit the sack."

Huneker walked to the front door with me, and followed me out onto the porch. We shook hands solemnly.

"Good luck, Huneker," I said gravely.

"Just how well did you know my wife?" he asked, frowning.

"To tell you the truth, my friend, I never even met her," I admitted.

"Then you had some kind of motive in coming around and pumping me. You planning some kind of interview story for the lousy newspaper?"

"Perhaps. Something like that."

"Print anything you like. I'm leaving Lake Springs and the whole damned state of Florida!"

"I always write what I please." I turned away, looking down for the first step.

"Here's some punctuation for you—!" As I snapped my head around I was just in time to catch a looping roundhouse right flush on my jaw. I tumbled backwards off the steps and landed on the lawn. The back of my head grazed a lawn sprinkler, and this gash hurt me more than the square, flat blow. Although I was a trifle dazed, I was a long way from being out. Rubbing my jaw, I sat up on the damp lawn. A trickle of warm blood ran down the back of my neck from the cut under my hair.

"I had that coming, Huneker," I said, grinning, watching him warily as I got to my feet. "Do you feel like going a few rounds out here on the lawn? Maybe you'll feel better if you get some of it out of your system? I can beat the living hell out of you, you know—and I'll be glad to oblige you."

Huneker laughed, a short, barking explosion, and I was willing to bet it was the first time he had laughed since Monday night. "No," he said, "not tonight. Some other time, maybe. I just gave you one for the road."

"Don't leave town without looking me up. Don't even try, because I'm going to keep tabs on you."

"I don't intend to."

"Good. For the kind of woman you're looking for, you won't have to be pretty. And I'll see that you aren't."

He didn't reply, but entered the house and slammed the screen door. There was a five-cent package of Kleenex in the glove compartment of my car, and I dabbed at the small cut on the back of my head. The cut wasn't serious; it didn't even burn when I moistened a fresh Kleenex tissue with whiskey and held it there till the bleeding stopped. Across the street, all of the lights began to come on in Huneker's house as he walked from room to room flipping switches. He even flooded his backyard with light. I waited a couple of minutes longer, and then the sound of the hi-fi blasted the quiet neighborhood as he turned it up. Now, I thought, maybe the poor bastard can get some sleep.

Chapter Fifteen

There was no reason whatsoever for me to return to the frowsty office, but I did. I had nothing to do there, and neither did any of the others—not really. That is, except for Dibs Allen, perhaps, who toiled away at his typewriter stringing cliches together about the football game played earlier that evening between the Lake Springs (High School) Rattlers and the Pebble Beach (High School) Bearcats.

Harris of the greenish face, his eyeshade pulled well down, was engrossed in a paperback novel at the slot, while he awaited the page-proofs to come up from downstairs. Mrs. Mosby, three long yellow pencils growing out of the blued coil of gray at the back of her head, was working on an inoperative adding machine with a screwdriver and a can of oil. And through the glass door of the M.E.'s private office, I could see the scowling little man at his desk, a soft pencil attached to his fingers, reading something or other. Only Blake, the Negro office boy, was doing anything worthwhile, and he was desultorily sweeping the floor with a well-worn pushbroom. So here we were, all of us, and on a Saturday night, sitting around in a dreary office trying to make work for ourselves.

Of course, Harris, Dibs Allen and Blake were bachelors; J.C. Curtis was a widower, and Mrs. Mosby was a widow—but why in the hell was I hanging around the crummy office? I was a married man with a wife and a child and a home...

Beryl, though, was at the theater (acting?). And if I went home I would be stuck with the babysitter, old Mrs. Fredericks, a lonesome widow, who would want to discuss the Civic Theater play in minute detail. So I sat alone at my littered desk, waiting, my thoughts as ragged as the dusty muslin curtains humping in from the window as they were caught by the breeze from the lake.

Jack Huneker. I thought about this simple widower who had to turn on every light in his home before he dared to go to sleep. In his simple way he had tried to reason out his wife's death, and had rationalized himself out of accepting the responsibility. And why not? As he said, he had a long time to live with himself, and life goes on and on and on. In time, Huneker would get married again and, in all probability, beget more children. But the statistics were against his finding the kind of woman he said he wanted. A widower almost always married the same kind of woman he had the first time, whether his first marriage had been a happy one or not.

Despite the fiction so beloved by American women, the male *always* chooses his own wife. And if he allows her to believe otherwise, it is only to keep from arguing. Jack Huneker would never be satisfied with any earthy widow, no matter what he thought. He was painfully romantic—and any well-brought-up American girl would cheerfully overlook his crudeness because he was a good "provider."

The riddle of Marion Huneker's murder–suicide job remained unsolved, and I didn't give a damn anymore. Something, and she didn't know what it was, had been missing from her existence, despite the fulfillment of her material needs. She had tried to find out what that missing element was, and failing, killed herself. What was it? Love?

Love. The overused word had lost its meaning, and yet, love meant something different to women than it did to men. And if I had learned nothing else during my halfhearted investigation, Marion Huneker had definitely been a feminine-type woman. Jack Huneker should have told her that he loved her every now and then whether he did or not. This was basic male knowledge; I had learned as far back as the tenth grade that if I told a girl I loved her the chances were that her pants would come down. Who was it, Dorothy Parker or Dorothy Thompson (Jesus! It couldn't possibly have been Dorothy Thompson!) who said a man could get anything he wanted from a woman by calling her Baby?

My SUICIDE SERIES envelope was full; notes, clippings, wire copy, and the carbon of my general article on suicide. I found Marion's manuscript in the bottom drawer, intending to reread it, but I couldn't get past the title. *Little Mrs. Little!*

This poignant title brought a couple of forced tears from my cynical eyes. Hell, I thought, as I brushed the rusty teardrops away impatiently, this little woman could easily be *any* housewife.

Even Beryl, my misguided Florida Cracker, was little Mrs. Little, in her attempt to act a difficult part in a meaty play—without any experience or training! And for what? For attention. To be noticed. To be loved.

Marion Huneker had written an unconvincing short story, and Beryl had played an unconvincing role on the stage, and both of them had attempted to do something in the creative line as a substitute for love.

This was as far as I got in my thinking when I heard J.C. Curtis call out my name as he approached my desk. His thirty-dollar Panama hat was pushed back on his bald head, and he was shaking a sheaf of copy paper at me. He glared down through his glasses, tossed the manuscript on my desk.

"This isn't what I wanted, Hudson," he began. "I didn't want any high-school treatise on suicide! I want a specific story—the facts behind Marion Huneker's murder–suicide. This is pap, pap, pap!" He slammed a small doubled fist into his open palm to make a slight slapping sound.

"I see," I said, standing up slowly and nodding. "Then you'd better write it yourself."

I dumped the contents of the suicide envelope into the metal wastebasket beside my desk. I flipped on my lighter, ignited the contents, and stepped back three feet to watch the cheery little fire. The basket had already been half-full of paper, and the fire blazed merrily away. Harris and Dibs Allen remained at their desks, but sweet little Mrs. Mosby came hurrying over, carrying a tiny paper cup of water she had filled at the cooler. Blake, for some inexplicable reason, took the red fire ax down from the wall and hesitantly advanced upon my desk.

"Let it burn, Mrs. Mosby," J.C. said curtly, waving his secretary and Blake away. "This is the first spark of incendiary action Hudson has shown around here in five years, and I want to enjoy it."

"Am I fired?" I asked, and I truly didn't care.

"No," J.C. said soberly. "I'd say you were fired up."

I pretended to warm my hands over the dying blaze. "In that case then, I want a transfer to the day shift. I'm a married man and I've been working nights too long."

"You start Monday. Report to Mr. Gladden at seven-thirty A.M. Sharp."

"Do you really mean it? Just like that?"

"Of course I mean it. Now I can get your persistent wife off my back. In the past month, your charming wife has phoned me at least a dozen times and visited me twice at my hotel with the same request."

The shaft of sudden anger that hit my stomach cooled before I had a chance to make angry retort. I grinned. "I'm sorry my wife bothered you, Mr. Curtis, but we thought you'd be more inclined to go along with the change if Beryl softened you up first."

"Uh huh," he commented, "you know it and I know it but I wonder if Beryl knows it." He turned away, adjusted his Panama squarely on his head, and disappeared down the stairwell.

After telling Blake to dump the charred contents of my basket I sat down at my desk again. I was bewildered by the swift turn of events. Why had I said that? I didn't want to work days—I detested Mr. Gladden, the City Editor—how would I ever finish my play?

But I knew in my heart that I didn't really care whether I ever finished my play or not. The only thing in this world that mattered was the working relationship between Beryl and myself. Without Beryl I could easily end up in an ascetic cell like Mr. Paul Hershey, writing stories for fifty dollars apiece because I didn't have any emotion…and I certainly didn't want to be all alone like Huneker—with only blazing electric lights and ear-blasting hi-fi music for company.

The time was eleven-nineteen, and I dialed the Civic Theater's backstage number. If I could manage to catch Beryl at the theater before she left for home we could still go out and have a few drinks together while the babysitter was with Buddy. We could have a gala joint-celebration; her success in *Lilliom* and my transfer to the *Evening News*.

Bob Leanard answered the telephone. "Hi, Bob," I said cheerfully. "This is Richard Hudson. Is my wife still around?"

"You aren't funny, Richard," he replied bitterly.

"I'm not trying to be funny. If Beryl's still in the dressing room I want her to wait there for me so I can pick her up."

"You honestly mean to say that you didn't know? I don't think I believe you."

"What are you talking about?" The genuine concern in my voice must have convinced him.

"She didn't show up, that's all. She phoned me a little after three this afternoon—too damned late for me to get anybody else up in her part—and said she didn't intend to play tonight. Just like that. No explanation, nothing. I asked her if she was sick, and she said, 'Oh, no, I'm just tired of acting, that's all.' And then she hung up on me. I tried to ring her back, but she wouldn't answer the phone. And we had a full house tonight, too! I had the stage manager walk through her part and read the lines, and it was God-awful! I'm telling you right now, and you can relay it to your wife! She'll never get another chance at a part here while I'm the director! And another thing—"

"Good night, Bob." I racked the phone, picked it up again, and dialed the first two digits of my home number before I hung up again. My hands were perspiring and there was an icy trickle down my back.

Woodenly, I left the office and drove home. I stopped automatically at red lights and full stops, and drove slowly and carefully. I had to get home, and I couldn't risk any delay because of a speeding ticket or any other traffic violation. I stubbornly refused my mind the privilege of any ordered thought.

I parked at the curb, rolled up the windows, and got out. The front door, as usual, was unlocked. Buddy, wearing light cotton pajamas, sat on the leather ottoman three feet away from the lighted television screen. He looked at me incuriously as I entered, turned back immediately to the screen. My throat was dry, and I realized that I hadn't talked to my son since last Monday—six full days ago!

"What're you doing up so late, son," I said, ruffling his hair.

"Watching Ghoul Theater," he said impatiently.

"Did your mother say you could stay up?"

"She didn't say I couldn't," he said defiantly, without looking at me.

"Where is Mother, Buddy?"

"In bed, I guess. She went to bed right after supper."

"Good night, Buddy." I switched off the set and looked away from the bright dwindling diamond in the center.

"Oh, Daddy…!" he started to whine. I jerked him to his feet and swatted him in the seat.

"Bed!"

"Yes, sir. Good night, Daddy."

Buddy went into the bathroom and I had a short drink of Old Indian. After I heard Buddy's bedroom door close I opened the door to our room and switched on the overhead light. Beryl was lying face down in the center of the wide bed on top of the sheets. She was wearing a shorty white flannel gown and it was hiked up well above her hips. In contrast to her brown, beautifully tanned legs her buttocks looked like white satin. I apprehensively felt those great white mounds with the tips of my fingers—and the flesh was *warm*! Beryl stirred, shrugging her shoulders, and I flipped her over on her back, using both hands, with one swift movement. And then she was awake and sitting up and her arms were around my neck and I was telling her again and again as I mumbled against her soft neck that I loved her.

"Say," she said sleepily, "what's got into you?" She grabbed a double handful of my hair and pushed me away, smiling in that dumb way she had.

"Oh, nothing," I said, fumbling in my shirt pocket for a cigarette. "Just thought I'd tell you I loved you, that's all."

"Did you think I didn't know it?" She kissed me, took the cigarette out of my fingers, and attempted to pull me down beside her.

"Why," I asked, a little hoarsely, "why didn't you do the play tonight? You knew they didn't have an understudy for you. Bob called me, and he was pretty well put in a spot."

"You aren't mad at me are you?" she said anxiously.

"Of course not. But I wondered about it. You know, the show must go on, and that sort of thing…"

"Well, I really did try to call you about it. Twice. But both times your line was busy so I made my own decision. You think Bob Leanard is a special friend of yours—well, he isn't! Last night, after the play, Les Wetzel, the stage manager, had a bottle in the green room. And he's a pincher, by the way, and don't let anybody tell you any different. Bob Leanard was there—we were all in the little green room—and three or four others. So we got Cokes out of the machine, and Les passed around the bottle. I didn't think you'd mind if I had one with them. After the play, a little drink tastes pretty good—"

"Sure, sure."

"Somehow the subject got onto you—how I don't know—and I was really shocked to think that they'd say what they really felt about you with me right there. They know I'm your wife! But Les was saying you didn't know anything at all about theater, and your reviews were a big joke and all. Then Bob Leanard, your friend, he said the biggest joke of all was the play you were supposed to be writing. He said he didn't even believe you were writing a play, at least he'd never seen it and neither had anybody else. I kept my mouth shut, just smiling and all, and then Marge Clouden, Ruby McKay's married sister, who's doing costumes—Marge, not Ruby—came in and offered me a ride home.

"Well, I was really mad about it last night. Here you've been writing all these wonderful things about the Civic Theater year after year and that's the kind of thanks you get! So this morning I got to studying about it, and the more I thought about it the madder I got. And I thought to myself, 'All right! They think they're so good and so smart; let 'em find out how they do when there isn't any Hudson around to carry 'em along!' So this after-noon I called Bob Leanard, told him I was quitting, and that was that."

The radiant love in Beryl's clear, gray, innocent eyes was so blinding I had to turn my head away with embarrassment. Beryl had grabbed a fat, juicy, acting plum that had been coveted by at least twenty other young women, all of them more talented in acting than she, and yet she had tossed it back in their faces for daring to criticize her husband! She wasn't even close to being Mrs. Huneker's understudy.

But from this moment on I was irrevocably Beryl's. So long as she loved me and was confident that I loved her, nothing else mattered. Beryl had a champion who was ready to defend her against the world, a man who was up in his lines and ready to go on for her at any time.

I resolved, then and there, that somehow, someway, I would be the man she really thought I was already—no matter what it cost me and no matter what happened.

Perhaps one of these days, I will even have a play running on the Broadway stage. I've got the incentive. God knows, I've certainly got enough incentive.

And besides, such things happen all the time—especially in the movies.

…yeah.